FINAL FANTASY XIV

Chronicles of Light

If you are reading this, then perhaps you, too, walk in the light of the Crystal.

I myself am something of an adventurer, though my deeds are of no consequence, and are surely not recorded anywhere. Nor less my name. Unlike most adventurers, though, I have been blessed with a mysterious power. The power to transcend the walls of the self—those born of emotion, of subjectivity, of the very body and soul.

The power of the Echo.

Of the myriad known manifestations, I possess the variety that allows one to walk in the memories of others—albeit not by choice. Rather, when in the presence of certain individuals, I have found myself unexpectedly transported into the midst of momentous events, all of which I have discovered relate at least tangentially to a singular hero.

The hero of the Scions and all of Eorzea. The slayer of false gods. I am sure you know of whom I write. I was aware of said hero's many accomplishments long before I deduced they were the common thread that linked these visions of mine, and realized why I had been blessed with this power: to chronicle that great journey and that still greater legacy.

This collection of stories is the culmination of my work. It is the product of my travels—the hidden history I strove to unearth through careful study of correspondence and journals, as well as the secrets known only to the heart and the mind. To discover these details, of which even the Warrior of Light must have been ignorant, has helped me to better understand how a single shining soul could brighten the lives of so many—and provided me with no small amount of joy besides.

Our hero's tale has been a source of untold inspiration to me, and it is my humble hope that you, dear reader, may find similar cause to dream in these most trying times…

CONTENTS

Tales from the Calamity

In the year 1572 of the Sixth Astral Era, the armies of the Eorzean Alliance and the Garlean Empire met in battle upon the fields of Carteneau. In the midst of that terrible carnage, weary soldiers craned their heads upwards and looked upon crimson Dalamud with horror as the lesser moon shattered and the elder primal Bahamut burst forth, an avatar of fury determined to lay waste to all and sundry. So ended an era, and the world as we knew it.

In the days preceding and following this calamity, brave souls steeled themselves for the challenges ahead, and it was thanks to their concerted efforts that Eorzea survived to see another day.

Tales from the Calamity

Where Victory and Glory Lead

We are lost, thought Merlwyb Bloefhiswyn. Immured for eons and free at last, the primal Bahamut laid waste to the Carteneau Flats, burning Eorzeans and Garleans alike. *But I will find a way.* Tearing her gaze away from the bloody churn, she bit down gently on her tongue—an old commanders' trick—and despite the ash-laden air, the voice that issued from her throat was as clear as compass wind.

"Belay previous orders! All Maelstrom units are commanded to fall back, effective immediately!" In the distance, the Admiral caught a glimpse of Archon Louisoix's resolute silhouette, arms raised in the rite of summoning. *Not even the Twelve can help us now*, she thought with something like despair as she swung herself into the saddle. *Dalamud has hatched, and no man can unbreak an egg.* "Give the Foreign Levy priority! Let the main host cover their retreat, and bring up the rear!"

Eynzahr Slafyrsyn let go the bridle as Merlwyb took hold of the reins. A shard of the false moon had pierced the mail under his right arm, she saw. Blood rilled, dark and steady. Her adjutant would likely not survive a hard ride. "Get those adventurers to safety," she repeated. "I shall send you stragglers. We must regroup—see to it!"

"At once, Admiral," Eynzahr snapped a salute. *He knows me too well to waste time arguing*, Merlwyb reflected as she urged her faithful bird to a gallop. *And he knows most of our runners are dead or near as, damn it.* A sharp "Kweh!" brought her back to the present. "Good girl, Vicki," she murmured as the chocobo sped onward through a blur of death and ruin.

"Fall back! Fall back to the main host!" Merlwyb called again and again until the rout became a stream, then a river, flowing towards Eynzahr and—she hoped—safety. But there was a knot in the crowd, fighting its way against the tide until it emerged at the rear, then pushing on towards the Garlean position. *Always*, Merlwyb thought without rancor and spurred her chocobo forward. *Always there are those who put glory before victory.*

"Save yer breath, Admiral. I mean to make those Garlean curs pay— an' pay they will!" Rhoswen spat, and Merlwyb was reminded of the old saying—*pirates weep with their swords, and their tears are red.* "So many Sirens… Spleeny Ebrill won't sing no more, nor Annest Blackeye, nor— There you are, ye liverless, tin-pot bastards!" A savage joy blazed in Rhoswen's eyes at the sight of something behind Merlwyb, and the Maelstrom commander touched her spur to Victory's left flank as she unholstered her pistols in one smooth motion. Death Penalty barked, and a Garlean legionnaire tumbled backwards. Two sharp coughs from Annihilator, and more men fell—to reveal the beetle-black gleam of magitek armor cresting the rise. *It has a beak*, Merlwyb thought with strange calm, her legs squeezing Victory's flanks of their own accord. The chocobo sprang as the magitek cannon roared. Then Merlwyb was falling, the world drowning in blood and feathers, and she knew no more.

"…The most rest you've had in years, I'll wager." Merlwyb awoke to a familiar sight: her quarters on the *Triumph*, and Eynzahr, his face graven with fatigue, but alive and on his feet.

"How long?" she demanded. "Present course and speed?"

"Two days, Limsa, eight knots," he answered. "The Alliance regrouped in Thanalan where the alchemists saw to our hurts. They meant to keep you abed in Ul'dah, but I assured them that would not be necessary. We are crossing the Strait of Merlthor for home."

"The Sirens? Rhoswen?"

Eynzahr laughed. Merlwyb could almost hear the rust in it. Command, especially the command of a retreating force, was a somber business. "The Bloody Executioners hauled you from the front like pullers with a bulging net, but they had no luck coaxing Captain Rhoswen to join the retreat. Then came the last of the dread pirate crews three, the Kraken's Arms, and Carvallain swept her up onto the saddle like a bloody knight of Ishgard. Last I saw, they were trading curses."

"Good." Merlwyb willed her eyes to stay open. She was suddenly very tired, and could not bring to mind the names of the others who had been present. No matter. Eynzahr would know. "The retreat from Carteneau—I ordered a unit be given priority. Did you get them to safety?"

Eynzahr looked at her, his brow furrowed. "Beg pardon, Admiral? My orders were to bring up the rear as the main host retreated, gathering any stragglers you directed towards us, then begin regrouping. You did not order that any be given priority over another."

11

The coming days were too full for Merlwyb or Eynzahr to fret overmuch about her odd lapse. She had taken a blow to her head, after all, and it was a trifle compared to what awaited them in Vylbrand. As the *Triumph* neared home, they saw livid crystals bursting from Pharos Sirius, flaunting their corruption for all to see. Galadion Bay was a floating Carteneau, the sea strewn with bodies, debris, and hollow-eyed survivors of the tidal wave that had scoured the coastline. *Eynzahr was lucky*, Merlwyb thought as she surveyed the destruction. *What size these shards, to make an eighth hell of this fair anchorage? And what of we who have been spared? How can we go on, when so much has been lost?*

I will find a way.

Merlwyb ordered that the Maelstrom's temporary command be established at the Moraby Drydocks, sheltered from the worst of the great wave by the Gods' Grip. From there, the remains of Limsa Lominsa's great armada sailed with food and supplies, aid and succor, women of strength and men of compassion. Admiral Merlwyb slept little, but when she did, it was always one of two dreams that she dreamed. In one, she bit down on her tongue, then called out, *Give them priority. Let the main host cover their retreat.* In the other, she rode a destrier in the cool night, the bird crooning contentedly and the rider murmuring, "Good girl, Vicki."

Time passed. Some wounds healed, others did not. The fishing boats returned to sea, and the merchants, stowadores, and cutpurses to the docks. The new Maelstrom Command took shape on the Upper Decks, the ships of the armada returned to their proper anchorage, and the Moraby Drydocks were recommissioned as a shipyard.

During those turbulent days, those who knew Merlwyb best—and they were not many—remarked that she had been changed by Carteneau. To the scores that came to the Admiral for help, she gave no false comfort, but neither was she as hard as once she had been. She spoke instead of hope, courage, and the lost warriors who stood with the Archon on the Carteneau Flats. For this Merlwyb won the love of her people, yet struggled to accept it. So unsettling did the thought seem to her that one night, unable to sleep, she wandered the city, finding herself at length outside an Ishgardian's stable as young birds murmured drowsily within.

When Naldiq & Vymelli's began work on the first of the thalassocracy's new warships, there was no question as to whom the honor of naming it would go. One fine day soon after, half the city turned out to see the *Victory*'s keel laid. When the Admiral of Limsa Lominsa inscribed her name upon the oak with a great flourish, the cheers rolled like thunder across the tranquil waters of Galadion Bay, and set the gulls and ravens flapping from every mast.

The Sultana's Seven

Nanamo watched from her private terrace as the Immortal Flames filed out of Ul'dah. The host left the city via the Gate of Thal—an egress symbolizing passage into the afterlife—in hopes of cheating death upon the battlefield. Crowds had gathered for the occasion, their boisterous cheers resounding through the sultanate, but Nanamo did not hear them. She stood transfixed before the balustrade as Raubahn put his spurs to his courser, and there she remained long after the dust had settled in the rearguard's wake. She had steeled herself for this moment, but when it finally came, she found that her courage had deserted her all the same. Suddenly, the reality of her isolation was only too plain, and the mere thought of it made her struggle for breath. *I am alone. May the gods grant me strength.*

As the days went by, the weight of responsibility and uncertainty began to tell. Nanamo's nights were sleepless. Not even her favorite dishes would pass her lips, and her round Lalafellin cheeks took on a hollow cast. Sure enough, despite the best ministrations of her ladies-in-waiting, her health began to fail. She became a ghost of herself, and her duties went untended.

Whenever a difficulty presented itself, she would invariably think, *If only Raubahn were here*, cursing her own weakness, even as the thought took shape. She knew very well that, as Flame General, Raubahn's place was with the host at the Carteneau Flats. It was his duty to lead his men into battle against the VIIth Imperial Legion. *I shall soon be six and ten summers old. I cannot rely upon others forever. Sooner or later, I must stand on my own two feet. I only hope I have the strength…*

Another meal came and went untouched. Taking her leave of the dining hall, Nanamo glanced apologetically at the silent shadow that was Pipin Tarupin, adoptive son of Raubahn and officer of the Immortal Flames. The earnest young soldier remained at her side at his father's behest, entrusted with her care in the Flame General's absence. Pipin would never admit it, dutiful as he was, but Nanamo knew that he would sooner be fighting beside his comrades at Carteneau. She could not help but feel responsible for denying him his wish—and for what? Though

Pipin was his father's son, it was plain to both of them that it was the father that she needed.

And so the days dragged on, each fading into the next, until the hour of reckoning came at last.

"Word from Mor Dhona, Your Grace! The battle is joined!" Nanamo was in the Fragrant Chambers, holding private audience with Thancred of the Circle of Knowing when Pipin burst in with the tidings. A weak "I see" was all she could manage in response. While Pipin strove to hide his disappointment at this tepid utterance, Thancred was quick to make his feelings known.

"Begging your pardon, Your Grace, but I had hoped for something a little more rousing." Since agreeing to serve as an advisor to the sultanate, the self-proclaimed bard had made himself at home at court, becoming ever more irreverent in the process. "When last I looked, your people had need of you."

"What could a powerless puppet like me possibly do?!" Nanamo snapped back, immediately regretting her petulance.

The bard was not discouraged, however, and responded with uncharacteristic force. "You are *not* powerless, Your Grace. You can pray for Eorzea's salvation."

Prayer? she thought. *Has it really come to that?* But of course it had. Even as they spoke, Dalamud drew closer. According to Archon Louisoix, only by the power of the Twelve could the lesser moon be returned to the heavens and the coming of the Seventh Umbral Era forestalled. And only by the prayers of the faithful could that power be summoned forth. It was to allow the summoning ritual to proceed unhindered that the soldiers of the Eorzean Alliance—Raubahn among them—now fought at Carteneau.

Thancred went on, his voice taking on a gentler tone. "If you pray, so too will the people. And the combined strength of their faith shall bear their plea for Eorzea's salvation unto the heavens."

A moment passed in silence. *If praying is all that I can do, then I will do it with all my heart.* Composing herself once more, she nodded, rose from her seat, and turned her steps towards Arrzaneth Ossuary.

Upon arriving at the temple, Pipin helped Nanamo to her knees and stood guard as she prayed. On the far side of the city, at Milvaneth Sacrarium, Thancred was doing the very same, she knew. *O gods of my forefathers, deliver us from destruction. O gods of my forefathers, bring Raubahn safely back to me.*

A few hours into her vigil, chaos erupted. The Ossuary shook violently, as if struck by a giant's fist, prompting Pipin to draw close as masonry fell about them. Terrified screams filled her ears, but Nanamo did not give in to panic. In defiance of the tumult around her, she prayed with all her being.

Her determination was soon rewarded. The stone plinth bearing the mark of the Dusk Trader began to glow. Moments later, a pillar of light burst forth from its surface, enveloping the image of Thal that stood upon it and illuminating every corner of the hall. In that instant, Nanamo felt the presence of the divine. Even as she basked in the sensation, a familiar voice echoed in her mind. "Let Eorzea be born anew," it said. *Louisoix*, she thought, and knew no more.

Nanamo awakened to find herself lying prone on the Ossuary's smooth stone floor. Footfalls rang out all about her. From the corner of her eye, she saw Pipin rise to one knee, seemingly struggling to shake off the selfsame torpor that gripped her. For a time she remained still, content to gaze up at the stone plinth. Its divine light had faded, she noted dimly.

A shrill yell brought her back from her reverie. "Rioters at Sapphire Avenue! They're headed this way!"

Consternation swept over Pipin's face. "Your Grace, we cannot linger! Let us return to the palace at once!"

"I will not hide while my people suffer!" The answer rose to her lips unbidden, with a swiftness that surprised even her. Rising to her feet, she surveyed her surroundings. Robed figures were scrambling hither and thither, bearing precious tomes and artifacts away, presumably to safety. At the heart of the bustle, a small yet commanding figure was barking out orders. Nanamo recognized him as Mumuepo, High Priest of the Order of Nald'thal and Master of the Thaumaturges' Guild.

"The rioters cannot be allowed to defile the Ossuary!" the man fairly screamed. "Incinerate any foolish enough to come near!"

These words set Nanamo's blood to roiling. "And you call yourself a man of the cloth?!" Checking her fury, she addressed all present. "Our citizens are in the grip of fear. They but want for a voice of reason to restore them to their senses. Who among you will aid me?"

Pipin stepped forward, as Nanamo knew he would. "Though I am but a poor substitute for my father, I live only to serve you, my sultana. Pray command me as you see fit."

Next came Papashan of the Sultansworn, followed by five thaumaturges of the guild—Lalafells all, and brothers besides. No more answered the sultana's call, however. *Only seven,* she lamented as she took stock of her volunteers. *But they will suffice. They must.*

With gritted teeth, Nanamo stepped out onto the stricken streets of Ul'dah. Of their own accord, her hastily assembled escort formed a protective ring around her, and together they trudged through the smoke and rubble. No matter where she looked, her eyes were met with scenes of carnage. A girl cried over the charred body of her mother. A man lay moaning, his legs crushed beneath a tonze of stone. Their plight wrenched her heart, but she could not stop for them. First she had to quell the unrest, else there could be no lasting relief. *I will return for you all. This I promise.*

As Nanamo's band reached Emerald Avenue, the mob of rioters came into view. Shops and homes had been ransacked in its wake, the occupants fleeing for their lives. Undaunted, Nanamo forged onward to within earshot of the advancing rabble, where she stopped, took a deep breath, and set about her task.

"Papashan! I must have their attention!" Nodding, the elderly paladin produced a blinding flash that staggered some of the rioters. Many, however, continued their rampage, oblivious.

"Thaumaturges! Light up the sky!" In unison, the five Lalafellin brothers let loose a warning barrage of spells overhead. Most impressive among these was the conflagration unleashed by the brother with the bandaged face. Those rioters who failed to take notice before did so now. Satisfied, Nanamo turned to Pipin. "Lend me your back."

21

With a booming voice that belied her size, Nanamo addressed the rabble. "Heed me, my beloved citizens!" she began. "The realm lies upon the brink of the Seventh Umbral Era. Yet so long as we live, we must not forget our compassion. Now is not the time to take from your neighbor, but to proffer him the hand of succor.

"The brave men and women of the Immortal Flames risk their lives that we might go on with ours. Would you have them return to an Ul'dah that has torn itself apart?" Looks of shame manifested upon begrimed faces. "I ask that you be strong. Give in not to fear and despair. If we join hands in common cause, there is no hardship that we cannot overcome. Together, let us tend the wounds of our nation—of our shared home!"

Hearing these heartfelt words from their sultana, the madness began to melt from the rioters' eyes to be replaced by the gleam of reason. Soon after, a semblance of order returned to the city, and organized relief efforts commenced in earnest.

Some days later, the remnants of the Immortal Flames trudged back into Ul'dah, entering the city by way of the Gate of Nald. Wounded and weary though the soldiers were, they yet had homes to which they might return. In the midst of rebuilding, Nanamo issued a decree stripping Mumuepo of all official titles and accompanying privileges. Though such an act would ordinarily have been beyond her authority, it was made possible owing to clever maneuvering on Pipin's part. Evidence of rampant corruption was found, with the high priest in its midst, and his order had no choice but to abide by the sultana's will. In place of the incarcerated Mumuepo, the five Lalafellin brothers were made joint masters of the Thaumaturges' Guild.

In the months and years that followed, Nanamo often revisited the events of that fateful day. *I am not powerless*, she would remind herself. *There are things that even a puppet might achieve.* If she could do her duty as sultana in the midst of the Calamity, she could surely carry out the task to come.

Tales from the Calamity

Of Friends Lost and Found

The battle was over, but none could say that peace had returned to Carteneau. The lesser moon—and the winged abomination that burst from
its belly—had visited devastation on the once-fertile flats, leaving naught
but a scarred wasteland for as far as the eye could see.

Matron have mercy... I have died and gone to the seventh hell.

"Elder Seedseer! Come quickly!"

Kan-E-Senna turned with a start, the sudden cry rousing her from a
moment's reverie. She forced her eyes to focus on the speaker; a young
Serpent, his armor caked with dirt and gore, beckoning with a bloodied
hand.

"My lady! There's something trapped beneath the steel beast!"

Mustering her strength, Kan-E-Senna joined the youth beside a
fallen magitek reaper. From beneath the wreckage, she could make out
the anguished groans of one tenuously clinging to life.

One of our own...? Crushed by the armor of a fallen foe? At the Elder
Seedseer's command, five soldiers joined their strength, slowly raising
the battered hulk to free the unfortunate soul caught beneath. Even
as the ponderous mass rolled aside, however, it became clear that the
survivor had sworn no oath of allegiance to the Twin Adder, nor any
company of the Eorzean Alliance.

Clad in armor of the same unholy steel as the magitek monster that
had entombed him, the Hyuran youth met Kan-E-Senna's gaze. Not yet
a man grown, there he lay, bloodied and battered on this godsforsaken
battlefield. *Nophica have mercy—he is but a boy. Forced into service against
his will, like as not—ordered to lay down his life for a cause he scarce
understands.*

A strapping Elezen Serpent stepped forward, seizing the youth's
shoulder with a mailed fist and bringing the edge of his jade-hilted blade
to the boy's throat.

"But say the word, my lady. The lad will feel no pain."

"Stay your hand."

Kan-E-Senna's voice was soft, yet stern.

"He may have fought against us on the battlefield, but the battle is
over. Now he is but a wounded child in need of care—care that none
save us can provide."

"A-aye, my lady."

The soldier hastily sheathed his blade, his expression carefully neutral. Taking up Claustrum, the staff of legend carved from arbor immemorial, the Elder Seedseer stepped forward and focused her thoughts on the wounded youth.

"O guardians of this land, let the breath of life sweep across this plain that it may mend this child's broken body, and bring succor to his wounds…"

What left Kan-E-Senna's lips as a whisper rose to echo across the flats. A gentle breeze broke the eerie stillness in the air, whistling as it swirled about the spot where the boy lay still. The tortured grimace on the youth's face slowly loosened. His eyes opened for a brief moment, then closed in peaceful slumber.

"The boy will live. Bear him to the rearguard and see that he receives rest and nourishment."

"As you wish, my lady."

For the next few bells—mayhap a full turn of the sun, she could not say—Kan-E-Senna walked the battlefield, tending to the wounded. Eorzean, Garlean, friend or foe, it mattered not. *These people cry out to me to ease their pain.* Threading her way through the carnage, she weaved the incantations that would close wounds and ease anguish, bringing solace to the suffering.

And yet for every one that she saved, countless scores were beyond saving. Looking out upon the bodies of the fallen, the Elder Seedseer proclaimed, "They gave their lives in the name of hope." *And hope forsook them*, came the silent reply. *They would never have come here if not for me.*

As leader of Gridania, a nation barely a stone's throw from Garlean-held territory, it was Kan-E-Senna who first reached out to her comrades in Ul'dah and Limsa Lominsa, setting in motion the events that would lead to the reformation of the Eorzean Alliance. A seeker of harmony in all things, the Elder Seedseer never had any wish to lead her people into a bloody conflict. *Serenity, purity, sanctity*—the virtues she held so dear were nowhere to be found on the desolate fields of Carteneau. Yet what other choice had there been? The prophesied calamity could not simply be ignored—not if Eorzea was to have any hope of a peaceful tomorrow. If there was even a chance that it could be averted, was it not her duty to try?

Alas, the task had proven beyond her. Dalamud had fallen, unleashing Bahamut's terrible vengeance upon the land, and now the Seventh Umbral Era was upon them. Despite her best efforts, Eorzea's dream of hope had given way to a waking nightmare.

Kan-E remained in Carteneau for several days, seeking out what few survivors remained and saving those that could yet be saved. Staring out over the wrack and ruin, she would often think upon the decisions she had made prior to that calamitous day. *Was their suffering and sacrifice inevitable? Was there truly no other way?* She could not say for sure.

Nor was her uncertainty limited to past events. By tarrying so long in Carteneau, was she not failing her people? Was her place not with them, back in Gridania? *They too are suffering.* On more than one occasion, she resolved to return to the Twelveswood, only to reconsider. Her siblings and fellow Seedseers, A-Ruhn and Raya-O, had stayed behind to watch over the forest, as did many skilled and compassionate Hearers. *I trusted them then. I must trust them now.* Those who sacrificed themselves on the battlefield had done so at her command. *Until I have done all that I can for them, my place is here.*

She pressed on, scarcely stopping to eat or sleep. In the faces of the men and women she saved from death and suffering, she found the strength to carry on. The sun rose and set, and one day blurred into the next. But toward the close of the first week, the search parties had begun to return empty-handed. Among the soldiers who had stayed behind to assist in the relief effort, morale was low. They had seen the corpses of too many of their comrades, and their thoughts turned inevitably to the friends and loved ones awaiting their return home.

I have asked enough of them. It is time.

Summoning her most senior officers to her tent, Kan-E gave the long-awaited order, "Begin preparations for withdrawal. We are going home."

After her men had dispersed, the Elder Seedseer stepped out onto the ravaged plain one last time. *My work here is not yet done.* It had always been there, in the corner of her mind, but she had been too absorbed in the healing of the wounded to act upon it until now. Tracing the tatters of her memory and the aetheric currents in the air, Kan-E-Senna scoured the battlefield. Minutes became hours, her search yielding naught but devastation. *I know it is here.* "Archon Louisoix—show me the way."

The words were still on her lips when she saw it. There, nestled in the lee of a blackened crag, rested the shattered remains of a staff.

Tupsimati.

Kan-E recognized the great staff at once. Even lying there in pieces, its power was plain. She could feel the aetheric energies that radiated from it as keenly as one might the warmth of the sun.

Quite how she had known that the staff had survived the elder primal's fury she could not say. Standing there, it almost seemed as if the Archon's benevolent hand had guided her. This thought served to lift her spirits, and she forgot her aching legs. *Your death shall not be in vain, my friend.* Though Louisoix's great wisdom was lost to Eorzea forever, at least those destined to carry on his legacy would have his most cherished relic.

The next day, Kan-E returned home, much to the relief of her countrymen. Gridania had not been spared Bahamut's wrath, and the return of the Elder Seedseer was a source of much comfort to all as they struggled to pick up the pieces of their shattered lives. *Strong they are in the face of such adversity, but the road ahead will not be easy.* While overseeing the reconstruction of her home, Kan-E-Senna was reunited with two members of Master Louisoix's Circle of Knowing who had stayed behind to lend their aid to Gridania in her time of need. One day, when the time seemed right, she approached them.

"Yda, Papalymo. My friends…"

Kan-E-Senna searched for the right words, but they would not come. Holding out an ornate box of rosewood bearing the mark of the Carpenters' Guild, she simply nodded.

"For us? Oh, Kan-E, you shouldn't ha—"

Yda's smile froze as she raised the lid.

"M-Master Louisoix… They said he was… But…but I hoped…"

Kan-E saw tears well up in the girl's eyes, and soon enough, her shoulders began to shake. Even Papalymo, not one for emotional outbursts, was unable to contain his grief. And so the three of them shared a moment of mourning for the fallen Archon.

The Lalafell was the first to compose himself. Clearing his throat, he proceeded to expound upon the relic and its origins, as much, Kan-E suspected, to distract as to enlighten. Tupsimati, he explained, was fashioned from stone engraved with ancient incantations and a treasured horn of bone passed down from antiquity. As his late master had told it, the staff was the beacon that would summon the Twelve down from the heavens and bring about Eorzea's deliverance.

"You have done us a great kindness, Elder Seedseer," Papalymo continued. "Though none save Master Louisoix possesses the power to wield Tupsimati, I shudder to think what might have resulted had it fallen into the wrong hands. You may rest assured that we will keep it safe."

"I…I don't have the words to thank you," Yda added. "If only Master Louisoix were here. He always knew what to say…"

Perhaps sensing further tears were imminent, Papalymo quickly pressed on, "My lady—now that you are safely returned to your people, it is time we took our leave. Would that we could remain here longer to assist in the rebuilding, but other matters demand our attention…"

The scholarly Lalafell then proceeded to explain that the Path of the Twelve and the Circle of Knowing were to be united as a single entity—an organization that would strive to realize the dream for which Archon Louisoix gave his life: peace in Eorzea.

The realm had lost its greatest champion, and the threat posed by the primals, the Garlean Empire, and who knew what else still loomed large upon the horizon. *And yet*, Kan-E thought as she looked into the eyes of the two Sharlayans, *with brave souls like these to defend her, there is hope for Eorzea still.*

"Whatever evils we may face in the days and years to come, know that Gridania will always stand with you."

Five years after that fateful day, the wounds left by the Calamity had begun to heal in the Twelveswood and the realm at large. In those rare moments when she was granted a respite from her duties, Kan-E-Senna would often reflect upon the path she had taken. *Do you watch us from above, Louisoix? Has Gridania—have I done your legacy proud?*

"Elder Seedseer—the Council requires your presence."

Kan-E turned about with a start. Before her stood a young Hyuran in leather armor of the purest white—one of the Keepers of the Entwined Serpent, the Elder Seedseer's personal honor guard, established in the wake of the Calamity.

"…My thanks. Pray inform them that I shall join them anon."

The young soldier nodded deferentially. As he turned to take his leave, their eyes met, and the memories—ever brimming beneath the surface—came flooding back to her, the images as vivid then as they were five years before. *We pulled him from the wreckage. He was but a boy, alone and afraid…*

"Wait—I will go now. Pray accompany me."

"As you wish, my lady." The youth gave a slight bow as he took his place by her side.

There are few wounds that time cannot heal. Even those who once stood across the battlefield as enemies, through effort and understanding, may one day find themselves standing shoulder to shoulder, the stoutest of allies.

Offering a silent prayer to Archon Louisoix and the friends she had lost, Kan-E turned her thoughts to the friends who now stood with her, and the countrymen who looked to her for wisdom and succor. *The true rebirth of this realm has only just begun.*

As the sun's warm light streamed through the leaves and down upon the path before her, Kan-E-Senna strode purposefully forward. *The greatest challenges still lie ahead, yet we shall rise to meet them—together, as one.*

Tales from the Calamity

The Walker's Path

White and red. A flurry of petals, falling upwards into the sky. *Like rain returning to the clouds.*

Please come back to me, Father. Please...

Incense and unguent. *I can't breathe...* She waited for the telltale rise and fall of his chest. Eyes closed, he looked as though he were asleep. Almost. *I am not ready to say good-bye.*

Burning. The desert sun baked the nape of her neck as she clenched her hands and stared at the liars.

Her father had warned her that Ul'dah was dangerous—that they must keep to themselves and avoid attracting undue attention. In the end, however, it was not an imperial agent who took his life, but a goobbue, freed from its magical fetters during a parade. An accident. *My fault.*

"I'm so sorry, Ascilia. I never thought... We never meant for..."

Her fault.

"I know this wrong cannot be righted, but I will make what amends I can, I swear to you."

Murderer. It had been their scheme. They would stop the goobbue and become heroes to the people. No one was supposed to die. *But you will. All of you.*

Yet F'lhaminn weathered her curses and held her tighter. *Even when it hurt you to do so.* And though the hatred that once filled her heart did not vanish, it gave way to another sensation—a warmth Ascilia once thought lost to her.

Mother. It was solely a means to maintain the fiction. Her father's Garlean spymasters still sought Ascilia for her father's betrayal, but no one would seek "Minfilia," an Ala Mhigan orphan adopted by an Ul'dahn woman seeking to fill the void left by her lover's death. *Just another lie,* she told herself. *Woven with the truth, but a lie nonetheless.*

And then, one day, it wasn't anymore.

"A nameday gift for my dearest Minfilia. Belated, I know, but in my profession, unexpected delays are only to be expected."

The thrum of conversation in the Quicksand had masked the bard's approach. Minfilia hastily put away the remnants of her reminiscence and turned to face him.

Perpetually passing by, Thancred had drifted in and out of Minfilia's life for years. He had been seventeen when they first met—five years her senior. *Or so he claimed.* His carefree demeanor belied many secrets, not least his skill with a blade. The manner in which he had battled the creature that slew her father was proof of that. Of course, he preferred a subtler approach when circumstances allowed.

"Minfilia?"

It is as much his name as it is mine, Minfilia thought wryly. He had all but chosen it. As they sat down together at the quieter end of the bar, she was struck by the intimacy of their collusion, and felt a flush creep up her neck.

The parcel she received for her eighteenth birthday contained a mythril dagger and a sealed missive. "From my mentor," Thancred explained. "The man responsible for transforming a Lominsan wharf rat into the paragon of virtue you see before you."

Minfilia cocked an eyebrow. "And how many maidens fair has said paragon deflowered since arriving in Ul'dah, pray tell?"

Thancred smirked and gestured to the missive in Minfilia's hands. *To whom do I owe the pleasure?* she wondered, unfolding the parchment. The words were written in an elegant, flowing hand.

"You have walked in the memories of others, have you not?"

She recoiled from Thancred, the parchment crumpling in one hand as the other sought the hilt of the mythril dagger. "What did you tell him?" she spat.

In a moment of weakness, Minfilia had confided in Thancred about her visions—fragments of the past she had started to glimpse a year before. No one else knew what she had seen. *Or that I have heard Her voice.*

If the bard was surprised by her reaction, he did not show it. "Read on," he said quietly. "All the way to the end. I ask only that."

"It is foretold that on the cusp of an Umbral Calamity, individuals blessed with the power of the Echo will appear," the letter continued. *"During the*

Sixth Umbral Era, when the waters rose to swallow the land, the twelve Archons who stood against the darkness each bore this blessing."

Minfilia looked up to see Thancred staring at her. He abruptly turned away.

"The histories paint a fanciful picture of these gifted souls. Through countless retellings, the Archons' deeds are become myth, their powers more akin to gods than men. However, there are two things of which I am now certain. First, their gift, the Echo, granted them the power to walk within the memories of others. Second—"

Though Minfilia knew how the sentence would end, her breath caught in her throat as she read Louisoix Leveilleur's next words.

"You have been blessed with the selfsame power."

After a time, she spoke. "He cannot be serious."

"He is," Thancred replied. For once, the bard's voice was devoid of affectation. "Master Louisoix believes that we are on the verge of an Umbral Calamity, and that your gift is the key to ensuring our survival."

Happy nameday, thought Minfilia numbly. In stunned silence, she listened as Thancred proceeded to reveal that he was in fact a member of the Circle of Knowing, an organization founded by his Sharlayan mentor to forestall the coming of the Seventh Umbral Era. He and his colleagues had been dispatched to Eorzea's three key seats of power to further this cause by any means necessary. *A liar*, she thought. *But that much was clear from the start.*

"How you choose to use your gift is your decision," he concluded. "You've no obligation to us, nor to the realm, come to that. But for better or worse, this is your legacy. You can no more run from it than you can from yourself."

She bit her lip. *I am not ready to face this.*
But I will.

Though separated by countless malms, Minfilia and Louisoix searched for answers together, but being no scholar, Minfilia sought knowledge via other means.

"There are more like me, but different," she wrote to him. *"We wander in the darkness alone, but if we came together and shared our experiences, we*

might yet come to understand the Echo—mayhap even to control it."

"A splendid idea, yet one fraught with peril," Louisoix warned. *"As you well know, men are wont to fear the gifted. Proceed with caution, my child, and do not allow your true intentions to become known."*

Minfilia could not help but smile. *This child is more experienced than you think.*

To outsiders, the Path of the Twelve was but one in a sea of obscure religious sects devoted to the pursuit of spiritual knowledge. Its charismatic Antecedent, the Lady Minfilia, led a small but devoted following of "walkers," so named for their resolution to walk the path with her. *A lie woven with the truth.*

The Circle of Knowing was of great help in those early days, particularly in identifying those who had woken to the Echo. Their ranks swelled, and two years after she had first learned the name of her gift, she began to educate others in its use.

And so the days passed—some more quickly than others. The order grew, and with it, its mission expanded. *As did the risks.* There were days of celebration; of sorrow; of waiting; of greetings and farewells… *And sometimes all of them at once.*

Nael van Darnus is dead. It should be over. Alone in the Hall of the First Step, Minfilia paced. Overhead, the lesser moon Dalamud continued its descent towards Eorzea, apparently indifferent to the demise of the Meteor project's chief orchestrator. *Can naught else be done?*

As if in answer to the question, there came a gentle knock at the door. The white-haired Elezen who entered was not quite what she had pictured when she penned the invitation. *He is older now*, she thought. *As are we all.*

"Archon Louisoix. It is an honor to meet you at last," she began. "Though now that I have said it, it feels…wrong, somehow."

"Indeed it does," Louisoix replied. As he held her gaze, a slow grin spread across the Archon's timeworn face, and the pair broke into stifled, then heartfelt laughter.

They spoke of better days and beloved colleagues, of exciting discoveries and shared accomplishments. It was natural. Unforced. *It is as if we have always known each other. As if we are family.*

Gradually, the conversation slowed. No longer could they postpone the matter at hand, for the hour of reckoning was upon them. "So…what now?" Minfilia began.

Louisoix shook his head. "Now we must part ways. Where I go, you cannot follow."

The Archon's plan was to summon the Twelve using forbidden arts known only to him. With their combined strength, he was certain that he could prevent the fall of the lesser moon. Such strength, however, posed a threat in itself. Should Eorzea's patron deities assume physical form, it seemed more than likely that they would be prone to the same appetites as the gods of the beastmen. Should that prove the case, their mere presence would bleed the land of life. And so Louisoix would instead call upon a fraction of the Twelve's power—enough to stay Dalamud's descent, and no more.

"It seems a fine balance to strike. Are you certain you can do it?"

Louisoix's voice was distant. "Mayhap not. But the Twelve cannot be suffered to set foot upon Eorzean soil." And then, head bowed, he told her the rest.

No. Minfilia shivered, suddenly feeling weak and cold. She had to fight the urge to rub her arms. "Is there truly no other way?"

"None half as reliable." He placed a hand on her shoulder. "If I do not return, the others will look to you. You must be prepared to lead them."

But I am not ready. She turned away, closing her eyes in a bid to stem the tears. "Do they know what you intend?"

"They know enough." He stepped forward. "Darker days lie ahead. But know that where there is darkness, there will always be light." His voice was soft and reassuring. *A father's voice.* "You will see the truth of this, Minfilia, when one who bears the light comes to stand before you. One who is gifted, like you. Together, you will greet the dawn."

Minfilia turned to face Louisoix once more. In the soft blue of his eyes shone cold steel. She held his gaze until she could no longer bear it.

Please come back to us. Please…

After the Calamity, Minfilia and Thancred summoned the surviving members of the Path of the Twelve and the Circle of Knowing to a joint meeting. As Minfilia shared the wishes of the late Louisoix Leveilleur, all present listened in quiet solemnity, and when she called for objections to the union, none were forthcoming.

"Henceforth, we shall be known as the Scions of the Seventh Dawn," she declared, and all agreed it was an apt name.

In times of trouble, she often gazed upon the fragments of Tupsimati, enshrined on the wall of her solar in the new Waking Sands. *What gave you the strength?* she wondered. *Who guided you through the darkness?* For five years she faithfully carried out his wishes—five years she kept the faith and believed in his words.

Five years spent working, watching, waiting. *But not in vain.* For when the adventurer entered the solar to greet the Scions, she knew at once.

I am ready.

Tales from the Calamity

In Louisoix's Wake

The ship glided out of the harbor, slowly gathering speed as its sails caught the brisk coastal breeze. Standing atop the quay wall with their father, Alphinaud and Alisaie bore witness to the vessel's departure—watched as Louisoix Leveilleur, their beloved grandsire, was carried away across the sea.

"And then he was gone." Alphinaud's voice was barely a whisper, his gaze fixed upon the dwindling form of the ship. Alisaie glanced at her brother with red-rimmed eyes but said nothing.

The twins had greeted the news of their grandfather's forthcoming journey very differently. While one accepted his decision with a calm practicality, the other had railed and wept. Still, to see the two of them there upon the quay, their slight arms hugging hefty grimoires as if their young lives depended on it, one would struggle to tell them apart.

They were not so different as they cared to believe.

"Even had you not gained admission to the Studium—and made me exceedingly proud in so doing—these gifts would have been yours regardless. Here—one for each of you. When read together, these two grimoires form a single tome. Provided you support one another's studies, I have no doubt that you will soon come to understand the lessons inscribed therein." The volumes Louisoix gave to his grandchildren scant hours before his departure were curious indeed. Crafted such that the contents of one could not be deciphered without the other, they hinted at the impish humor that danced behind the ofttimes solemn visage of Sharlayan's preeminent sage and scholar.

"Thank you, Grandfather." Alphinaud accepted his grimoire with a practiced grace and dignity. Alisaie, meanwhile, received her gift distractedly, and swiftly resumed her attempts to dissuade Louisoix from his course.

"Must you leave, Grandfather? Is there naught I can say to make you stay?"

"Please, my dear. We have spoken about this."

It had been almost a month since the twins first learned that Archon Louisoix would be leaving Sharlayan for the shores of Eorzea. His purpose, he had patiently explained, was to aid the distant realm in forestalling the ruinous arrival of the Seventh Umbral Era.

Sensing the fixity of his grandsire's resolve, Alphinaud had chosen to swallow his melancholy and voice no word of complaint. Not so his sister, nor less his father, Fourchenault. Alisaie protested the journey purely out of her abiding love for Louisoix and the unbearable thought of his absence; Fourchenault's strident objections were of a more political nature. Louisoix's eldest son was an influential member of the Forum, the body responsible for shaping Sharlayan policy, and he, like so many of his colleagues, was a staunch opponent of military intervention. It was, he believed, the duty of his countrymen to chronicle world affairs, not to interfere in them.

When the steel-clad wolves of the Garlean Empire descended upon Ala Mhigo, it was Fourchenault and his fellows who had attempted to parley a peace. In the bitter wake of the failed negotiations, however, they saw no recourse but to forsake the colony they had built within the borders of the war-threatened realm. Following five years of elaborate and painstaking preparation, the plan to evacuate the settlement's entire population to the northern archipelago of their homeland was put into motion.

In the year 1562 of the Sixth Astral Era, the city of Sharlayan—a renowned center of learning, situated in the Dravanian lowlands—became an uninhabited shell in the space of a single night. The twins knew that they themselves had taken part in this exodus, but could claim no recollection of the momentous event, being less than one summer old at the time.

"War is the favored resort of the uncivilized and the ignorant, Father," began Fourchenault, seeking to launch his own sortie upon the heels of his daughter's plea. "The wise abjure it. As Sharlayans, it is our task to observe—to *chart* the course of history, not to change it. Civilization shall not be advanced through petty conflict, but by the passing of recorded knowledge from generation to generation."

"My mind will not be changed, Fourchenault," Louisoix responded wearily. They had had this conversation, almost word for word, perhaps a dozen times in as many days. "To ignore the plight of those one might conceivably save is not wisdom—it is indolence. And such a passive stance will not, I fear, take us far upon the path to progress. That you would spare these younglings the horrors of war is a decision with which I am in full agreement. Thus do I refrain from exhorting you, or any other, to return to Eorzea at my side. We must all protect that which we hold most dear in the manner of our own choosing." And so the discussion ended as it always did, with neither willing to deviate from the script of their oft-rehearsed play.

Alphinaud and Alisaie, it must be said, were children of exceptional intelligence. So advanced were they in their studies of aetheric theory and other such esoteric subjects that both had gained acceptance to the Studium at the tender age of eleven.

Thus it was that the sharp-minded Alphinaud, while able to recognize the logic of his father's arguments, could also see that his grandfather's cause was just. That the boy remained silent then stemmed not from simple stoicism but from a keen sense of his own inadequacy—a realization that his unpolished skills would yet prove more a hindrance than a help to Louisoix's endeavor.

Though no less bright, Alisaie eschewed her brother's affected maturity, and gave vent to her discontent, inwardly cursing Alphinaud all the while for his mute acceptance of their grandfather's decision. *How can he stand there and say nothing?*

A small yet conspicuous crack had appeared between the siblings.

It was long after Louisoix had taken ship and vanished over the horizon that the fateful day came. Alphinaud and Alisaie were crowded into the Studium's observatory, along with their professors and a throng of fellow students. The assembled sages and would-be scholars huddled around the base of the giant telescope, each taking their turn to gaze upon the looming spectacle of the red moon, Dalamud.

"Dalamud has shattered!" Alisaie cried out, pressing her face closer to the telescope's eyepiece, so that it dug into her cheek. The view provided by the device's array of magnifying lenses was distorted and indistinct, but the fate of the satellite was unmistakable—she could see its crimson-fringed silhouette breaking apart in the skies over Carteneau.

"Shattered?! What…before it struck the ground?!"

"How is that possible?!"

Excited murmurs and hastily formed theories erupted from teacher and pupil alike.

"He's done it! Grandfather has saved Eorzea!" Alisaie turned to find her brother's face, her eyes glistening with tears of joy and relief. For some time now, Archon Urianger had been kind enough to relay to them brief reports of Louisoix's efforts in those chaos-stricken faraway lands. It was he who had informed them of their grandfather's presence at the Carteneau Flats, and of the battle that still raged like as not beneath that bloodred sky.

Shouldering aside his madly grinning sibling, Alphinaud squinted through the ocular lens. Though the air was thick with billowing clouds of smoke and ash, he was forced to agree with Alisaie's assessment—Dalamud was no more.

But something is awry… Alphinaud continued to scrutinize the distant scene. The red moon's bloody glow had been replaced by an equally unsettling incandescent rain, as if the heavens themselves were weeping tears of light. *Terribly, terribly awry…*

Dalamud's spectacular demise gave rise to a tidal wave of aetheric energy that rendered linkshells all but useless for a period of many days. During this time, the Leveilleur siblings were left to stew upon the wonders they had viewed from afar. Then, after weeks without word, a letter from Urianger arrived.

The Archon's elegant script described horrors the twins could scarce bear to picture. From the cracked husk of the red moon had emerged a dragon primal immense beyond imagining—an incarnation of wrath and raging flame that had laid waste to the land for malms in every direction. Undeterred, Louisoix had persisted with his plan to call forth the power of the Twelve, and thus, it seemed, was the abomination banished. Eorzea had been saved.

When the siblings reached the conclusion of Urianger's staggering account, however, the pale flame of hope that both had been nursing was finally extinguished.

On the broken fields of Carteneau, did my dearest mentor—thy beloved grandsire—become as light and embark upon his final journey.

Alphinaud's shoulders trembled with quiet sorrow, while Alisaie wailed aloud, caring not who heard her grief.

Five years later, a ship once more glided slowly out of the harbor. Alphinaud and Alisaie stood on the gently rolling deck, watching the gradually shrinking figure of their father, alone upon the quay.

Recent graduates of the Studium, the twins were now sixteen summers old—old enough to be considered of age in Sharlayan society. And so, although he opposed his children's planned journey, Fourchenault had not sought to bar their way.

"And now it is our turn," murmured Alphinaud, thinking back to the day of their grandsire's departure.

"We follow in Grandfather's wake," replied Alisaie, her head bowed.

Looking over at her, Alphinaud was struck by how widely their convictions differed. As they gripped the rail, however, identical grimoires now hanging from their belts, one could hardly tell them apart.

No, they were not so different as they cared to believe.

Tales from the Dragonsong War

The Warrior of Light. The savior of Eorzea. A hero beyond reproach. Or so we thought. Through betrayal and intrigue, he and his comrades were named as the assassins responsible for a sultana's death. Driven to ground, they sought refuge in the northern city long closed to outsiders—the Holy See of Ishgard.

Man and dragon were still locked in their thousand-year war when he and his passed through the the city's great gates. On that fateful day a new chapter in his tale began, one that would be marked with fortuitous meetings and bitter partings alike.

When he looked on those towering spires and the heavens above, I wonder…what did he feel?

Tales from the Dragonsong War

Vows Unbroken

The wind nipped at the young man's face as he trudged up the path towards the stones, fresh lilies clasped tightly in hand. *Another blizzard on the way*, he thought. *The worst is yet to come.*

All too soon, he arrived. As he knelt to replace yesterday's offering, Francel's eyes drifted to the shield leaning against the marker. A red unicorn, erased and wreathed in thorns. And below…

He shuddered, and looked away. "You just couldn't help yourself, could you?" he muttered through clenched teeth, twisting and crushing the flowers in his hands until there was nothing left.

Fifteen…sixteen years now, Francel reflected. *A boy of six summers, yet nevertheless old enough to assume his social responsibilities.* Father had told him the dinner party at Fortemps Manor was to be the first of many.

The lords and ladies had treated him with predictable kindness as he made his rounds with the count, carefully repeating the phrases he had been taught. "This one is a baron, but you mustn't address him as such in person," his father whispered as they moved on. "That one is sworn to our house. You met him when you were…"

It was altogether too much.

But he pressed on, as instructed, until he had spoken with every individual of standing. Utterly spent, he duly begged his father for a moment's respite and was surprised to find him amenable to the request. *Moved by my efforts—or mayhap the wine.*

After the count set him free, Francel made straight for the doors, pausing only to snatch a serving of pudding from a nearby table. Outside, under the starry sky, he breathed deep of the cool night air and savored the silence.

"Come! Have at thee! For the glory of House Fortemps!"

The shouting seemed to be coming from the nearby gazebo, where Francel had hoped to eat his pudding in peace. He crept closer, unsure what he would find.

A silver-haired boy twice his age was swinging a wooden sword with reckless abandon, his bare chest glistening with sweat in the moonlight.

"What are you doing?" Francel was surprised to find he had spoken. The older boy whirled about, briefly falling into a half crouch. He blinked, then drew himself up to his full height. "What does it look like? *I'm practicing!*"

Francel was at a loss. His father had stressed the importance of the evening's festivities. "But... The party... Shouldn't you be—"

The older boy snorted. "The countess forbade it. Father wanted me to come, but I told him I wasn't interested. It's just as well—what good's a knight who can't fight?"

It was better when I didn't know. Trueborns, bastards, baseborns...

The older boy simply stood there, hands resting on the pommel of his wooden sword, point planted in the earth. Francel suddenly remembered the pudding in his hands. "Would you like to share?" he said, proffering the sweetmeat with trepidation.

Haurchefant arched an eyebrow, then grinned. "I would like that very much."

They complemented each other rather well. *So far as a fourth-born and a bastard could.* Quiet and reserved, Francel's inclination was ever to bury himself in a book, but Haurchefant was wont to appear without warning and spirit him away on some grand adventure. Six years his senior, the older boy continued to pursue his study of swordplay, spurred ever onward by his dreams of knighthood. *For we all must serve, each in our own way.*

In later years, Haurchefant's impromptu visits grew more frequent. *The more he grew to resemble his father.* Francel came to recognize the signs he would be along shortly—muffled shouts from the manor, a door slamming shut, the patter of running feet across the cobbles.

And there he was, huffing and puffing, eyes red and full of anger. I'd touch his shoulder, and he'd remember where he was. "Where shall we go today?" I'd ask. "Anywhere but here," he'd say.

He shifted in the saddle and kept his eyes firmly fixed on the horizon. The trackers were off watering their chocobos, leaving Francel alone with his father, who continued to speak.

"Many of your peers are avid falconers, you know. And with good cause—not all bargains are struck over wine. Out here, in the wilds, astride a chocobo, men are more like to speak with candor…"

To celebrate his eleventh nameday, his father had insisted they go hunting in the eastern lowlands. *Father always had a way with gifts.* Glancing at the trackers, Francel saw a shock of silver hair and smiled, before returning his attention to the skies. *One small concession, at least.*

The black speck in the fading daylight had begun to circle above the woods on the far shore of Clearwater Lake. He felt the count squeeze his shoulder. "You see? All you have to do is follow the falcon. He knows where to go." The count paused, then turned to face him. "He was born for this—as were you."

The falcon's cry was a blessing. "He's got something!" Francel yelled, then dug his heels in and spurred his mount forward. He was dimly aware of his father shouting as he gripped the reins tighter and urged the chocobo on.

If there's one thing Haurchefant managed to teach me, it was how to run away. Francel grinned as he lowered his head and rode light in the saddle. His father's men would not catch him before he made it to the trees.

When he was nearly upon them, a flock of pheasants burst from the underbrush. *Towards me.* Francel reined his mount in, puzzled, and squinted into the gloom, only to feel a sharp pain in his head. And then he was tumbling from his saddle while the world went black around him.

He awoke with a start to a dull throbbing at the base of his skull and the taste of blood and cotton. Moaning, he tried to reach up and feel his head, but found that he could not. *Sawdust and hemp. Oh how it chafed.*

"Oi, the little lordling's awake!"

Gradually, the world came into focus and Francel found himself lying on the floor of a candlelit cabin. *A woodcutter's shack, long abandoned and forgotten.* The door on the far wall appeared to lead out into the night… but sat on a stool across from him was a balding man in boiled leather, with a nose that had been broken at least half a dozen times and teeth that had fared still worse.

The man leered. "My mates was afeared I hit you too hard, but I told 'em blue blood skulls're thicker'n you'd think." A knobbed wooden club lay across his knees. *An ugly, misshapen thing, not unlike its owner.*

Francel tested his bonds once more, and the coarse rope bit into his wrists. He tried to speak through the gag. "Quiet, boy, or I'll send your tongue back to the count before your fingers," the man growled. *An empty threat, but how was I to know?*

Horrified, Francel pressed himself against the wall and stared up at the bandit, who smiled. *And was all the more terrifying for it.*

"That's better. Now then—"

The door flew open, and the bandit rose to his feet and whirled about, club in hand, just in time to catch a glimpse of the silver-haired youth who barreled into his chest, dashing him to the floor and driving the wind from his lungs.

The bandit clawed at Haurchefant's face, spitting curses as the youth fumbled his knife. Beyond, in the doorway, a man was lying flat on his back, staring into space. *Unblinking.* Haurchefant groped blindly for the knife, found it, then drove it home between the larger man's ribs. *Again and again, long after he had stopped moving.*

He lay there for a time, face buried in the dead man's chest. The cabin was silent save for his labored breaths. *Less a man and more a beast, his tunic dyed red, his hands trembling.* Slowly, he pushed himself up and looked into Francel's eyes. "It's over. They're dead," he whispered, leaning forward and pulling the wadded cloth from the boy's mouth.

"All of them?"

A man filled the doorway, arrow nocked and drawn. "You little shites!" he roared, and the bowstring sang.

I shut my eyes, but I heard it strike—heard him howl, heard the pounding of the floorboards. Heard them wrestling, two voices grunting…then one wheezing…

When he opened his eyes, Francel saw Haurchefant kneeling next to a third bandit. "Right. *Now* it's over." He rose to his feet, swaying slightly. A thin stream of blood trickled from the broken shaft embedded in his left forearm. He looked down and almost seemed surprised. "Best not try that again without a shield, eh?"

The third one lived to tell the tale, Francel mused, as he traced the sigil on the battered shield. *Of how an untrained, unseasoned bastard of seventeen summers saved a lordling with naught but his knife. And so the Silver Fuller won his spurs.*

His fingers came to the hole.

"A knight lives to serve—to aid those in need," he managed, his voice trembling. Beyond the descending veil of white, the city rose to meet the day as Francel, kneeling in the snow, smiled and wept.

Through Fire and Blood

A gasp escaped his lips when he saw them—leathern wings too numerous to count, beating rhythmically overhead. For a blessing, the dragons showed no interest in him, a lone shepherd boy tending a flock scarcely worthy of the name. No, their sights were set upon something more substantial, and they continued on their course towards... *Oh no.* Dread gripped him like a vise. He broke into a run, half bounding, half rolling down the hillside. Regaining the trail, he followed it east, where the dragons were headed—to the village.

After what seemed an eternity, the boy stumbled onto the muddy thoroughfare. All the way, he had told himself that the village might be spared, that the dragons had designs on some other place, but now the truth asserted itself. Devastation spread out before him. Piles of splintered wood and rubble lay where houses had stood, while haystacks, sodden from the recent rains, spewed forth plumes of white smoke. Though his chest was ripe to burst from his headlong dash, seeing the carnage imbued him with a desperate energy, and he broke into a run once more. Though the acrid fumes choked his lungs and stung his eyes, he did not slow his pace. *Please, Halone! Please let them be safe!*

The Fury did not hear him. Rounding a corner, his heart caught in his throat as the remains of his home swung into view. The roof had fallen in on itself, bringing one of the walls down with it. Passing the splintered fence, he found his parents. His father's arm lay across his mother as if shielding her from the wind, but the scorched earth told a different story. Though a deathly numbness had begun to overtake him, his legs continued moving of their own accord, taking him inside the cottage. There, he discovered his younger brother sprawled upon the floor, his body obscured by fallen masonry. His face was untouched by the violence, his expression serene. At a glance, it appeared as though he was simply asleep and would open his eyes at any moment. He would have given anything for it to be so.

All hope extinguished, the boy's strength finally deserted him, and he fell to his knees. With a trembling hand, he reached out to stroke his sibling's snow-white hair, tears drawing pale lines upon his soot-blackened cheeks. But the sorrow soon gave way to rage. He cursed Nidhogg and his brood for taking from him all that he held dear. And he cursed fate for condemning him to live on.

"Wake up! You weren't among the fallen, as I recall!" A commanding voice tore Estinien from his nightmare. He found himself propped against a rocky outcrop. Through blurry eyes, he made out a male silhouette. His head swimming, he mumbled the first name that came to mind, that of his adoptive father and mentor.

"Al…Alberic?"

"Nay, friend, alas," the figure replied. "We would have fared better had he been with us. Here, drink this and clear your head."

Estinien gratefully accepted the proffered skin and gulped greedily, the water soothing his parched throat and restoring his senses. Pausing after a long draft, he stole a glance at the dark-haired man crouching next to him. His armor identified him as a fellow Temple Knight. By his reckoning, they were of an age, no more than a few years past twenty. Estinien had seen him before, but he had no name to put to the face. Since joining the order, he had always been something of a lone wolf, spurning contact with his comrades in favor of honing his skill at arms.

"My thanks, Ser…" Estinien began.

"Aymeric, and you are quite welcome," the dark-haired knight responded, a hint of amusement in his voice. Glancing over his shoulder, his tone became grim. "I fear we are the sole survivors."

Regaining his wits, Estinien scanned his surroundings and stifled a gasp. The scorched field was strewn with the bodies of a dozen knights, their armor blackened and their flesh fairly cooked. In an instant, it all came back.

He and his unit had been dispatched to Ever Lakes in response to a dragon sighting. As they traversed hilly terrain, a massive red beast had descended upon them. Half perished in its searing breath before they could even draw their weapons. Leading the counterattack, Estinien had succeeded in wounding and repelling the dragon, only to succumb to the smoke. Though the air had now cleared, the stench of burning grass still lingered. *Fuel for that accursed dream.* The remembrance, together with the scene of carnage, stoked the fire in him that ever smoldered—vengeance. *Such pain as I have suffered, I shall visit upon them a thousand times over.*

Estinien turned his attention to Aymeric once more. "I have a knack for surviving." *Whether I will it or no.*

He clambered to his feet. A wave of dizziness swept over him, and he nearly found himself back on the ground. Shaking it off, he picked up a lance to replace the one he had lost. Satisfied with its point, he turned to leave. After a moment of puzzled silence, Aymeric called after him, "The Holy See is the other way."

"You are free to head back," Estinien replied simply. "But I mean to finish what we've started."

"You mean to go after the beast alone?! That's tantamount to suicide! Besides, we have no way of tracking it!"

A knowing grin played upon Estinien's face. "Ah, but we do. Behold," he said, gesturing to a trail of blood. "From the blow I dealt to its underbelly." With that, he spun upon his heels and strode away before Aymeric could utter another word of protest.

For hours on end Estinien walked. The sanguine trail led him across hill and vale, forest and plain. At length it descended into a ravine, where it suddenly veered off and disappeared into a cave. Estinien took a deep breath and entered, his eyes gradually adjusting to the gloom. About a hundred paces in, the cave opened into a chamber. And there, at the far end, he found his quarry, its scaly form curled up tight. *I shall show you a nightmare such as you showed me.*

Estinien drew his lance, checking his grip once, and again for good measure. Then he charged. The flurry of footfalls roused the dragon, which reared in fury and bellowed a deafening challenge. In the next instant, a stream of swirling flame burst forth from its maw. Anticipating this, Estinien dove clear of the withering heat, rolled, and regained his feet within striking distance. Unerringly, he thrust at the dragon's wing, tearing through the leathery skin, and was rewarded with a pained howl.

"You'll not escape me again!" Estinien roared. But his foe had no intention of fleeing. No, it craved his blood more than ever, and came after him with a vengeance. So began a game of cat and mouse.

The dragon lashed out with fire, fang, and claw. Using the lay of the cavern to his advantage, Estinien succeeded in evading the worst of its wrath, striking back when the opportunity presented itself. And so the dance continued for a time, with neither side able to gain the upper hand. Eventually, however, the rigors of battle began to tell on Estinien, and his lance grew heavy in his hands. *Must end this quickly…*

As it turned out, the cavern itself would be the first to succumb. Shaken by countless wayward blows, a cluster of boulders came loose and rained down upon Estinien without warning. Though he managed to fling himself away in the nick of time, he found his footing scant yalms from his foe. *Too close.* The dragon's tail caught him full in the chest, sending him flying into the cavern wall. He crumpled to the ground, the breath knocked out of him, and lay there limply as his foe closed in to administer the killing blow. *Lucky bastard.* His vision already darkening at the edges, he clung to consciousness, and willed his body to move. But it would not obey.

An instant later, the dragon loomed over him, its molten eyes steeped in hatred, and time seemed to slow. He watched helplessly as the beast filled its lungs, and stared into its maw as fiery death welled up within and began creeping towards him. But just when it seemed certain that he would be engulfed, the creature's head lurched sideways, spilling fire everywhere and nowhere. Estinien did not pause to wonder why.

Summoning what remained of his strength, he leapt into the air. And at the height of his leap, he became as one with his lance and descended, tracing an arc worthy of the Azure Dragoon himself. With the full force of his weight, he came down upon his foe. The beast shuddered, collapsed to the ground, and was still.

Half in a daze, Estinien took in the sight of the first dragon he had ever slain. Only then did he notice the arrow protruding from one of its eyes. Moments later, a familiar figure emerged from the shadows to stand beside him, a longbow in hand. Estinien frowned.

"This is not the way to the Holy See."

"I know. But I thought the journey home would pass more swiftly in good company."

"You have my thanks, Ser...?"

A wry smile formed on his savior's lips. "Aymeric. And it shall be thanks enough if you remember my name... Though I shan't object to a tankard of ale back in Ishgard."

In spite of his exhaustion, Estinien could not help returning his grin.

Tales from the Dragonsong War

What Remains of a Knight

Ser Vaindreau de Rouchemande, the Very Reverend Archimandrite of the Heavens' Ward, was a man plagued by doubt.

Now well into his seventh decade, his body had long since begun a daily protest against the physical demands of his office. Yet it was not the constant aching of his knees nor the niggling twinge in his back that troubled the knight, but his faith in the man he had sworn to protect. For the first time in over forty years of service, Ser Vaindreau questioned the righteousness of the archbishop.

It had all begun a month before, on a morning like any other. He had been standing guard at the entrance to the Vault's inner courtyard, a haven of tranquility where His Eminence Archbishop Thordan VII was wont to meditate in solitude. The elderly warrior had kept many such vigils whilst the archbishop communed silently with the divine, and was thus startled when he caught the faint murmurings of conversation from the gardens within.

Praying aloud, Ser Vaindreau reasoned. But at the sound of a distinctly different voice, his hand found the hilt of his sword. Only the fear that he had somehow misheard prevented him from charging into the courtyard there and then. Cursing both his failing hearing and stubborn pride, he opted instead to edge forward as quietly as his clanking plate would allow.

Craning his neck to see past the flowering creepers, he sought about for an intruder, and all but lost his balance when he espied his master in hushed conference with a man in black robes.

A Paragon.

First Inquisitor Charibert Leusignac had never been a patient man. Though his was a divine calling, he could not help but curse the sparsity of heretics upon whom to practice his craft. The unannounced entrance of his most incompetent apprentice did little to improve his mood. The boy shuffled in startlingly, his body seemingly in disagreement with his feet, shooting nervous glances about the chamber as he came. Finally, after fixing his gaze somewhere below Charibert's chin, he gingerly proffered an envelope.

"And this is?"

Plucking the missive from the novice's quivering hand, Charibert noted that neither the parchment nor the featureless wax that sealed it bore any hint as to the identity of the sender.

"A man in black robes gave it to me. He offered no name..."

And you did not think to ask, he observed silently, his lip curling as he imagined how he would punish the boy. Still staring at him, Charibert extended his index finger towards the seal and conjured a tiny tongue of flame, melting the wax but leaving the parchment unsinged; a reminder of his skill as a pyromancer—and torturer—not lost on his apprentice.

When the heat had done its work, he drew forth the letter with a flourish, his severe expression gradually giving way to one of unholy glee as his eyes danced back and forth across the page. A divine calling indeed.

Gazing out over Ishgard from the highest battlements of the Vault, Ser Vaindreau scarcely felt the icy sting of the night air upon his cheek. For what felt like the hundredth time, he asked himself what it was to be a knight of the Heavens' Ward...only for the rote reply to chime in as it always did.

We are the champions of the Holy See. We embody the virtues of the knights twelve who fought alongside King Thordan against dread Nidhogg. We are the chosen guardians of the archbishop, keeper of the one true faith. The Fury's shield and Her spear both...

But the creed said naught of an archbishop who consorted with the servants of chaos! He had heard the man discussing the finer points of a summoning ritual—intent not on calling forth Halone, but another. And although the exact nature of this blasphemous deity had escaped him, he knew that even to contemplate such an act violated the Church's most sacrosanct law.

There was naught else for it: he would confront the archbishop with the truth of what he had witnessed. And though he be condemned for heresy himself, he would hold Thordan to account.

Turning his back to the sleeping city and the last of his doubts, Ser Vaindreau descended into the deserted depths of the Vault, arriving all

71

too soon at the doors to the papal residence, where Ser Hermenost stood watch.

"I must speak with His Eminence on a matter of utmost import."

"The hour is late, Archimandrite. What dire tidings are these that cannot wait until—"

Ser Vaindreau silenced the younger man with a gesture of his hand, indicating his unwillingness to speak further with a single shake of the head. And though entry was strictly forbidden to all, Ser Hermenost stood aside—for this was no interloper, but the archimandrite of the Heavens' Ward. Closing the doors behind him, the old knight let out a quiet sigh of relief, and, after pausing to clear his thoughts, pressed on into the silence of the entrance hall. As he neared the gloomy doorway beyond, however, his eyes made out the shape of a hooded figure.

"Who goes there?!"

Though he barked the perfunctory challenge, his every fiber screamed the answer—*the Ascian!*—and he squared up to the shrouded phantom, barely conscious of having drawn his sword.

"'Tis past your bedtime, ser knight. Whither art thou bound with such haste?"

The figure threw back its cowl, revealing features split by a twitching smirk. Marking the man's severely tied-back hair and predatory gaze, Ser Vaindreau needed only a moment to identify the intruder.

"I will ask the questions, First Inquisitor. Your office does not permit this trespass!"

Though relieved that it was no Paragon that stood before him, Ser Vaindreau did not relax his grip on his weapon. Charibert was a man of sinister reputation, and the knight instinctively gauged the distance he would need to cover to put the grinning mage within sword's reach.

"You know of me, Archimandrite? I am honored!" Charibert replied, his unctuous tone eliciting a wince of distaste from Vaindreau. "As for the matter of my 'trespass,' why, that is easily explained," he continued. "The inquisition received certain intelligence that a heretic would seek to pass through this very hall on this very night, and thus was I granted leave to lie here in wait."

At this revelation, Ser Vaindreau's grim expression grew darker.

"You imply that *I* am suspected?"

The knight knew not how his actions had been anticipated, but there could be only one reason the man he had served faithfully for four decades would invite such a viper into his house: the archbishop wished him dead.

Though his tired mind reeled at the revelation, Ser Vaindreau was nevertheless one of Ishgard's finest warriors. When the flames came, he was already hurling himself away from their blistering heat. He rolled to his feet with a clatter, and barreled forward with shield upraised.

Charibert, a seasoned war mage himself, clucked his tongue in annoyance, and calmly intoned another spell.

"Burn, heretic!"

A fiery sphere burst forth from the tip of the inquisitor's ornate staff and exploded against Vaindreau's shield. With reflexes honed by a lifetime spent battling dragons, the veteran flung aside the rapidly melting lump of metal and lunged with his blade in one fluid motion.

"Hmph. For all your creaking, you do your order proud, old man." Though a timely backward leap had saved his eye, Charibert bled freely from a cut running down his right cheek.

"You think to claim a knight of the Heavens' Ward with such feeble fires?!" Vaindreau raged. "A clean kill may be your intent, but you spare the stones a blackening at your own peril!"

The inquisitor had indeed been holding back, meaning to boil the aged warrior inside his armor without leaving a mark on the marble. And now it seemed his miscalculation would prove his downfall—the last exchange had left him with his back against the wall. He would have no time for lengthy incantations. Yet even though every advantage now lay with his opponent, he could not help but smile.

"How fine it is to fight a wolf after so many sheep," Charibert purred. "I shall remember you with fondness, Ser Vaindreau."

The following morning, somewhat earlier than was his wont, His Eminence Thordan VII emerged from his chambers. Beyond the entrance hall, a sleepless Ser Hermenost yet stood at his post, while Ser Vellguine de Bourbagne waited patiently to accompany the archbishop to morning mass.

"Ser Vaindreau came to me last night to announce his retirement," Thordan announced in a quiet voice.

"Beg pardon, Your Eminence? He said naught of— The archimandrite has *resigned*?"

The archbishop nodded gravely. "As a man past the prime of life, he confessed the burdens of knightly service had begun to take their toll. We spoke at great length upon this and many other things until the small hours of the morning..." Thordan glanced back towards his residence. "Ser Vaindreau now takes his rest in the antechamber, and I would not have him disturbed. We old men need our sleep."

Emotions warred across the faces of both Ser Hermenost and Ser Vellguine as they contemplated how such a decision must have pained their pious commander. Of any knight living, Ser Vaindreau had been the staunchest advocate of the Heavens' Ward and its sacred duty. But what was done was done. Leaving their comrade to his most well-deserved rest, the two knights took their places at the archbishop's side and departed for the cathedral.

Some few days later, the Holy See officially announced the retirement of Ser Vaindreau de Rouchemande from the Heavens' Ward, and introduced Ser Zephirin de Valhourdin as the order's new archimandrite. Addressing Ser Vaindreau's conspicuous absence at the anointment ceremony, the archbishop explained that the knight had begged leave to depart on a pilgrimage—a final wish for peace and solitude that the Church could hardly deny.

And thus did the Heavens' Ward lose its last true champion, his passing marked by little more than a faint scorching that yet mars the cold stones of the papal residence's entrance hall floor.

Tales from the Dragonsong War

The Dreamer and the Dream

Such a tiny thing, Ysayle thought as she cradled the crystal in her palm. *Like the purest water turned to ice…* She squeezed it with all her might and then slowly opened her hand. Turning her gaze to the heavens, she sighed and continued onward.

Across the cracked cobbles and up the ancient steps. *When last I walked this path, I was not alone.* Through the ancient arch and over fallen stone. *The defender, the diplomat, the dragoon…and the dreamer.* Past the spinning aetheryte and towards the winding ramp. *How far we traveled…and all for naught.*

"'Tis but a shade conjured by thine own fancy."

Zenith was where it had all come to an end—where her beloved had named her an impostor and a fool. Where her companions had turned their backs on peace.

How desperately we yearn for that which we have lost.

"Hear… Feel… Think…"

She had sought refuge from the snows in the Dravanian forelands, and while wandering those unfamiliar fields had been chanced upon by the great wyrm Hraesvelgr, descended from the heavens to hunt. *Or was this too somehow Her design?*

Through his memories she had glimpsed the truth behind a thousand-year lie. *An eternal requiem sung for his murdered sister. What could I do but speak out?* And so, after years of hushed half-heresies, of coded missives and midnight gatherings, she had gained a flock. *"Redemption is not beyond us, my friends! Come and hear the truth! Come and hear the Lady Iceheart speak!"*

"Spread the truth and cast down those who concealed it. I was so certain that would be enough…"

"Men have ever been fond of lies."

Ysayle felt Hraesvelgr's eyes upon her as his voice resounded in her mind, each word a dagger through her heart. She could not bear to look.

"I had to believe…"

She knew not what the Ul'dahn's intentions were. *But we are come too far to turn back now.* And so the bargain was struck, and the merchant furnished them with the supplies and the information they required. While the lord commander and his allies celebrated their victory, they would finish what Vishap had begun. *And so we did.*

Fire and blood. And screams…so many screams. Mine own join the chorus, calling for order, calling for justice…but there is none to be had. Men fight, men run, men die—without reason, without logic. I speak, but they do not listen. I see the girl, no more than ten, hiding amongst the rubble. The wyvern sees her too. I beg. I plead. I pray…

I pray.

At last, she spoke. "I twisted your memories into a fantasy of mine own creation to further my selfish dreams."

"Is this why thou art come? To beg forgiveness?"

"No," she replied, raising her head to meet his gaze. "I am come to atone."

As I came before, with the ones I thought mine enemies. They who were truer allies than any in the hate-filled Horde…

"I would go to them—to the Warrior of Light and the others. I would aid their cause once more. But I know not whither they have gone…"

The great wyrm regarded her silently for a time. "The dragoon beareth my brood-brother's eye to Azys Lla…and its twin."

"So you *can* sense them," she said, with a hint of accusation. "I beseech you, then: deliver me to my comrades. Let me join in their fight!"

Hraesvelgr bared his teeth ever so slightly. *Was that a smile?* "Such power was never meant for man. Yet ever shall he covet it. Hast thou the strength to deny him his desire?"

She felt for the familiar angles in her pouch, drawing comfort from the crystal's coolness. *Such a tiny thing.* "I have," she said at length. "Lend me your wings, Hraesvelgr!"

Scarcely had she uttered the words when she found herself in a mind not her own.

In azure skies we soar, her laughter music to my ears. As I fold my wings and turn into a dive, she clutches me tightly, pressing her face against my back. "Lend me your wings," she had asked, though they are hers to command. My gentle Shiva—

Ysayle blinked. The great wyrm's expression was unreadable. *He knows.* Hraesvelgr lowered his head and she clambered onto his back without a word.

I spread my wings, tense my legs, and push... Yes... I remember...
She tried desperately to forget.

The hours slipped by as the skies grew dark and cloudy. In the distance, a light shone. *That light should portend such darkness...*

Hraesvelgr's voice came to her. "He draweth upon the Eye's power."

As they drew closer, she could discern a small airship at the center of a mass of swirling aether. The reddish-black maelstrom grew in intensity, accompanied by a rising hum, then suddenly winked out as the sound of breaking glass echoed around the heavens.

"We must hurry!" Ysayle yelled, straining to be heard above the cacophony. "Below them, look!"

A massive Garlean battleship rose from the depths and positioned itself behind the smaller airship. In an instant, the air was thick with cannon fire.

No... not like this. Not like this!

"The time is come to use Hydaelyn's gift," she whispered, drawing the crystal from her pouch. "Much blood has been spilled in my name. And for what? For a false cause that I created for want of the warmth of companionship." She clutched it to her breast and felt the cold seep into her skin. "Saint Shiva... Hraesvelgr... Pray forgive this fool. But even now, I cannot let go of my dream—my dream of a tomorrow in which no child need freeze alone in the snow."

With a roar, Hraesvelgr bore her high above the battleship. With a breath, Ysayle closed her eyes and let go.

Never again would I harm another, I swore. Never again would death stain my conscience...

Ysayle felt him slip away as she fell and a thousand thousand fires blossomed around her. Slowly, she opened her eyes. "Thank you, Hraesvelgr." *And forgive me.*

And then she spoke.

"O goddess born of mine own hopes and dreams. For the last time, I beseech you! Fill this vessel with your light! Still the hatred within our hearts and bless us with eternal grace!"

The crystal melts into light, and we are whole again. Warm. My mind grows cloudy, my essence faint, but I hold fast to the memories.

In azure skies we soar once more...

Words, Deeds, Beliefs

"When I set out to master the dragoon's jump, 'twas not to strike fear into the hearts of high-hanging fruit."

Alphinaud chuckled as he remembered Estinien's ennui.

In the days since the dragoon vanished from his sickroom, he had found himself with an overabundance of leisure. Catching himself mindlessly tracing the patterns on the ceiling of his room at Fortemps Manor, he closed his eyes and let out a sigh. *Another sleepless night.*

Resigned, he rose from his bed and walked over to the great oak desk. Sinking into the chair, he reached for the leather-bound journal he had begun writing a lifetime ago. *When I saw my arrogance and vanity for what it was—then, in the very depths of my despair—he spoke to me.*

"Are you content to remain a broken blade? Is there no flame hot enough to reforge you?"

Mayhap not. A flush crept up his neck as he closed his eyes and recalled the kind words Lord Haurchefant had spoken to him, and the brave face he had put on at the time. *Old habits.* And then they had left behind the Falling Snows and embarked upon the journey that would change everything. *Even me—albeit slowly.*

Though the whole of Eorzea looked to the adventurer as a hero, to Lord Haurchefant the great Warrior of Light was above all else a friend. And the feeling was plainly mutual. *Kindred spirits.* Like the Warrior of Light, the knight lived to serve. To protect. To sacrifice. *For there is no greater calling.*

Though he had welcomed them both with open arms, it was only later that Alphinaud came to understand the true depth of the knight's love for his friends and for his nation. How it would save them, how it would save him. *Too late.*

Accordingly, in the peaceful interlude following the war's end, he had returned to the memorial atop the cliff overlooking the capital, and there said to the north wind all he had failed to say before.

Opening his eyes, Alphinaud returned his gaze to the journal which lay before him and began to turn the pages. Instantly, his mind was transported back to the time when the four of them, each from different walks of life, had taken to the road on an impossible journey.

"How lightly you propose the destruction of this god. Has it occurred to you that you may be sending the Warrior of Light to their death?"

Estinien's words had stung more than a slap to the face. Only his grandfather or Alisaie could have been so blunt. *What would you have said, dear sister, had you been there to hear me, the supposedly reformed commander of the Crystal Braves, blithely send another in my stead, having so recently resolved to fight my own battles?*

And still they fought. And still they fought… And if they resented me for it, I would not blame them.

Alphinaud had found himself pacing while they waited for Ysayle and the Warrior of Light to return triumphant from Loth ast Gnath. In that eternity, Estinien had watched him, sometimes stone-faced, other times wearing a strange expression. *They will come back to us. They always do…*

Alphinaud Leveilleur. Words were his weapons—his intellect, his reason, his wit. *Grandfather's gifts to me, like all else.* Alphinaud Leveilleur. There but for the name did men hearken to him—respect him. *What have you wrought by your own hands?*

Alphinaud. *Not a man who sacrifices his friends and family for a cause, but one who fights with them—fights for them.* Anything less would be empty words and hollow promises.

"Master Alphinaud possesses a rare talent for the arcane arts. Should he continue to apply himself to their study, he will become a formidable mage in time."

Though he had trained in the martial applications, it had ever been purely as an academic exercise. But with Ysayle's encouragement, he had resolved to pursue a more practical education. *Mayhap not today, nor even tomorrow, but one day…one day I will stand at your side.*

Alphinaud turned the page, and his breath caught in his throat.

We have made camp in a clearing not far from Zenith, and on the morrow hope to meet with Hraesvelgr. Ysayle saw to our evening repast, and all agreed that her stew was the finest we had ever tasted. I, for my part, gathered the requisite firewood, taking care to remember Estinien's instructions…

Some part of me still labors to believe that we have come this far. That we have treated with dragons…and even a distant tribe of moogles! And that Estinien did not give the latter a thrashing. Then again, had he tried, the Warrior of Light would inevitably have intervened. Would that I had such strength and courage.

Until some few moons ago, I was supremely confident of my own abilities—convinced of my own superiority—only to be shown, all too clearly, how ignorant and powerless I truly am. I said as much, earlier, when we were gathered around the fire…

In the end, Ysayle received my confession rather more sympathetically than I had expected. "We all of us are guilty of a similar ignorance," she told me.

What matters, then, is that we strive to replace our ignorance with knowledge, while remaining true to our convictions.

If only it were that easy…

A soft rapping drew his eye from the journal to the doorway, from which a sliver of lamplight slowly widened.

"Master Alphinaud?"

Closing the journal, he rose and turned to acknowledge the former count.

"It seems I am not the only restless soul this night," Edmont smiled. "Personally, I find that a warm cup of herbal tea can oft work wonders at such times. Would you care to join me in one?"

"I would be honored."

As they made their way towards the kitchens, Alphinaud shared some of the thoughts born of his insomnia with Lord Edmont, who nodded understandingly. Upon arriving, the nobleman refused the assistance of the sole manservant present, instructing him instead to deliver extra blankets to the Scions' chambers. Lord Edmont then set about heating the water and preparing a mixture Alphinaud did not immediately recognize. When asked, he explained it was made from the roots of Nymeia lilies.

86

"A difficult plant," Alphinaud observed.

Lord Edmont smiled faintly and said nothing.

They enjoyed their tea in silence. Several times Alphinaud thought to speak, but found himself unsure of what to say. And then the cup was empty.

"I must thank you again for your most generous hospitality," he finally began.

"Full glad were we of your company," came the reply, with a promptness that took Alphinaud aback. "May the Fury watch over and keep you safe on your journey."

He knows.

Gently setting down his cup and saucer on the table, Lord Edmont met his gaze and smiled. "You are a good man, Alphinaud Leveilleur," he said, and left.

Alone, Alphinaud refilled his cup and took another sip. *A bitter draught.* Wincing, he reached once more for the honey, but stopped when the dancing fragments of Nymeia lily root in the tea chanced to catch his eye.

Seated at his desk once more, Alphinaud returned to his journal and the memories contained therein. At the sight of the words "Falcon's Nest," he shuddered. *That I should live to see the emissaries of dragon and man meet—only for the promise of peace between their peoples to be torn asunder by the avatar of their vengeance.*

The dragoon's crimson armor was unmistakable, as were the massive, twitching eyes fused to his arm and shoulder. In one fluid motion, Ser Aymeric snatched up the bow, drew, and loosed an arrow straight at the heart of his dearest friend. *He knew what needed to be done and did it. And in that instant, I knew that I could not.*

Nor could the Warrior of Light.

So we laid hands on those hideous things and pulled. Pulled with all our might, even as our bodies cried out in agony. And when our arms faltered, and our hopes faded, whence came the strength to wrench them free?

For those we have lost. For those we can yet save.

"Where once I craved vengeance, I now crave rest."

The sickroom was empty when they returned from Ser Aymeric's investiture, save for a vase of Nymeia lilies and the crimson armor Estinien had forsworn. *For all his protestations, he had not the strength to suffer heartfelt thank-yous and tearful good-byes.* And so it was that Alphinaud Leveilleur once more failed to say what was in his heart—failed to thank a man who cared not a whit for his name nor his station. *A man who treated me harshly but fairly. A true friend and comrade. A brother.*

In the morning, Alphinaud set forth, journal in hand, on a pilgrimage to retrace his steps throughout the north. Traveling alone, he was waylaid by bandits and beasts on occasion—but he was not the boy he once was, and easily defended himself with now well-practiced magicks.

After a time, he came once more to the peak of Sohm Al, and then to Zenith. He remembered the time he first stood before Hraesvelgr, how the earth had shaken when he descended from the heavens to weigh man's worth. He remembered the great wyrm's words and everything they had set in motion. *The Aery. The Vault…*

And so Alphinaud came again to Azys Lla.

There, at the landing's edge, he spied a bouquet of Nymeia lilies. *Estinien.* He had no way of knowing, and yet he knew.

We four, each from different walks of life, who took to the road on an impossible journey… Whatever else we may have been in the beginning—in the end, we were friends.

And we will meet again.

Closing his journal, Alphinaud finished his herbal tea and retired to bed. After taking a moment to stretch, he clasped his hands and rested them on his chest, turning his drowsy eyes heavensward. Before sleep claimed him, a thought came unbidden.

A bouquet of lilies for those we have lost. And for the living…
He knew.

As Alphinaud lay there, he could not help but smile.

Tales from the Dragonsong War

Thoughts Unspoken

Be present, yet unobtrusive. Predict, but never presume. Head bowed, ears open, stepping softly, he was ever ready to serve, as he had for nearly five years. Though well liked by his peers, to the lords and ladies he was but another nameless face among five score and more men and women who labored tirelessly for House Fortemps. *But your day will come—for do we not live in changing times?*

The end of the Dragonsong War was only the beginning. The manor had since seen an endless cavalcade of esteemed personages, eager to pay their respects to the old count and earn the favor of the new. Yet not all were so calculating—the newly elected representatives of the Commons seemed less interested in playing the great game and more in simply learning its rules. *Poor sods.*

Rounding the corner of the manor hallway, the manservant found himself face-to-face with the head steward of the household.

The old wolf grinned. "Ah, there you are. Walk with me. There is a delicate matter which I would entrust to no other."

"O-of course, Master Firmien!"

He listened in a daze as his superior listed the legal documentation that served as proof of House Fortemps' historical claim to Camp Dragonhead, which the count apparently required for reasons Firmien did not disclose. Pausing at a window, the steward clasped his hands behind his back and inclined his chin towards the noonday sun. "You should arrive before nightfall if you leave now. And lest there be any lingering uncertainty: you are not to return without those papers. Do I make myself clear?"

The manservant swallowed and gave an earnest nod, when a figure in the courtyard below chanced to catch his eye. Even at a distance, the adventurer was unmistakable. *Slayer of Gods. Rider of Dragons. Savior of Ishgard.*

"Master Firmien, is that not the Warrior of Light? I was told they would be staying with us for a time."

"I am given to understand that they mean to make a journey of remembrance—inspired by one of your compeers, no less. Let us pray you both return to the manor ere long."

The western sky burned crimson at the manservant's back as he was shown into the great hall at Camp Dragonhead. There, the knights listened patiently as he detailed his task, and he was duly granted free rein to search the stronghold for the requisite documents.

It soon became plain that his task would be far from simple. For all Lord Haurchefant's many fine qualities, the late commander of the garrison had plainly not been one for paperwork, his approach to the administrative aspects of his role apparently having amounted to stuffing reports, schedules, and invoices into the drawers of his desk at random. Nor were the young pages any help, as none had even the faintest idea where their master might have kept documents of greater import, if not in his office.

With a sigh, he called for ink and parchment. *Your day will come. Just you wait…*

Out of respect, the manservant had refrained from searching Lord Haurchefant's private chambers on the first evening, but after a fruitless night, he requested they be unlocked on the morrow. Alas, they too yielded naught. His hopes were further dashed at midday, when a raven bearing the head steward's simple reply arrived. *Don't ask questions you don't want answered.*

And so the manservant remained at Camp Dragonhead, scouring every location in which the documents might reasonably have been stored—and many more in which they should not. As the days wore on, he began to entertain elaborate fantasies as to their fate. *Mayhap a pack of highland goobbues wandered through the gates unseen and…no—a goblin thief! Yes, a goblin thief would have little difficulty hiding a hundred such documents in his pack's many secret compartments…*

Secret…

In the twilight hours of yet another sleepless night, the manservant made his way to Lord Haurchefant's private chambers once more, lamp in trembling hand. At once his eyes were drawn to the desk.

He found the drawer with the false bottom almost immediately.

"Fury be praised," he whispered as he fumbled for the papers within. There was no mistaking the seals. As he pulled them free and began to leaf through them, an envelope slipped between his fingers and fell to the ground. He knelt and saw it bore no markings. It wasn't even sealed… Intrigued, he set the other documents on the desk, picked up the envelope, and extracted the parchment within.

Oh…bugger.

My dearest friend,

I pray this missive finds you in good health and high spirits.

It has been some several days since you and Master Alphinaud embarked upon your journey to the west, having learned of the impending Dravanian invasion. Of course, I have no way of knowing when these words will reach you. Mayhap these troubled times will be but a distant memory when they do.

I realize that matters of great import command your attention at present, but when I looked to the distant skies the other day and found myself praying for your safe return, I felt compelled to put pen to paper. Do forgive me this indulgence.

Well then, what to write. I would ordinarily ask if you had been enjoying your time in Ishgard, but given the circumstances of your coming, and your subsequent embroilment in yet another battle not your own, mayhap it were better that I did not. I imagine it is by now altogether too familiar a tale. Even so, it pains me to say that it is distressingly easy to imagine you fighting to the bitter end regardless…

Nevertheless, I cannot deny that it filled my heart with joy to see you finally set foot in our fair city. The thought that I would be able to witness your daily feats of heroism firsthand was quite simply… Well, let us say that I was tremendously grateful for it. And the idea that I might once more fight by your side seemed no less thrilling!

Ah, yes, I have been meaning to say—I do hope my (likely misguided) decision to name your home away from home the Falling Snows did not grate. It was but my artless attempt to raise your spirits. When you sought us out in your hour of need, and I saw firsthand how utterly despondent Master Alphinaud was, I knew at once that I must do everything in my power to help you to preserve the dawn's light, be it as a friend (with a jest) or as an ally—which is why I resolved to petition my father on your behalf.

It was, to be frank, no easy thing for me.

Lest you mistake my meaning, my father is an honorable man, good and true. Doubtless that is why my late mother fell in love with him. Mayhap that is also why she thought it best to leave the family's service—that in doing so, she might help preserve his reputation, though she ultimately chose to place me in his care.

He loved her, of course, as I am sure he loves me, and I him, though we rarely speak of such things. But then our conversations are invariably rather brief.

Mayhap that is why I chose to become a knight.

Alas, my father was firm in his refusal, for although he had supported our shared endeavors with Revenant's Toll and the Scions in the past, providing safe haven for wanted fugitives was another matter altogether. Still I persisted, prompting my father to ask what could possibly have driven me to fight so fervently on your behalf.

And so I told him of the adventurer who had unexpectedly come into our lives—a bright, shining paragon of virtue, whose very presence drove others to be better than themselves. I told him that this adventurer, this cherished friend of mine, was a hero, lies and slander be damned, and that as their friend, it was only right that I help them.

Looking back, it may well have been the longest conversation we had ever had.

Afterwards, he simply stared at me in silence for what felt like an eternity. And then, when I had all but resolved to take my leave, he told me he would give me his answer on the morrow.

The rest, you know.

Thanks to you—and indirectly my father—I have come to appreciate my visits to the manor all the more. You are rarely there, of course, given your propensity for disappearing off on grand adventures, but I forgive you on the grounds that most are undertaken on our behalf! Truly, your famously calm disposition notwithstanding, I suspect, given the right encouragement, you would have some decidedly colorful observations to share. I should be honored to lend an ear someday—mayhap over a drink!

But you will think me facetious. Pray then allow me to speak plain.

My dearest friend, in whom I trust without hesitation, without doubt—

Come what may, I know you will strive on.

You will strive, and in the end you will triumph, on this journey and the next, and the next, and the next.

And when you have fought the good fight, only to find, yet again, that it is not enough—

I will be there.

This I promise. This I swear.

Beyond darkest night waits a new dawn. I pray you greet her with a smile.

Your friend,
Haurchefant Greystone

The fresh snow crunched underfoot as the manservant trudged up the path towards Providence Point the following day.

Eyes bleary from lack of sleep, he had set out upon hearing that the Warrior of Light had passed through the camp less than an hour ago. *Still on that journey of theirs.* Though the snow conspired against him with every labored step, he forged on, mindful of his task, for the envelope pressed against his burning breast.

Cresting the hill, the manservant slowed as he caught sight of the figure just beyond the standing stones. As he withdrew the unsent missive from his coat and approached, he opened his mouth to call out, only for the words to die in his throat.

The Warrior of Light knelt before the memorial, motionless. Even at a distance, the manservant could make out their face, a mask betraying nothing... And then, with soldierly abruptness, they rose to their feet, a curious smile spreading across their face. *You know, don't you? Everything he never had the chance to say...*

In that instant, the north wind laid claim to the letter, plucking it from the manservant's hand and spiriting it away into the heavens. As he craned his head upwards and shielded his eyes, he saw it spiral higher and higher and higher, until at last it was swallowed by the distant sun.

Tales from the Calm

As the Warrior of Light moves, so moves the world—for weal or for woe. Yet for his undeniable influence, the fates of friend and foe alike are often dictated by forces outside his control. Each is the hero of their own story, and seeks meaning and purpose in their own way.

Their tales too belong to the tapestry that is our hero's journey.

Tales from the Calm

For Coin and Country

Nanamo did not learn of the circumstances surrounding her strange slumber until three days after she had awoken.

It was Papashan who finally unfolded the truth to her. Though the retired Sultansworn was no longer her bodyguard—a position he had held since the sultana was a child—he had never quite relinquished the role. At first, Nanamo could do little more than listen to each shocking revelation in stunned bewilderment. But when Papashan described the loss of Raubahn's arm, and the accusations leveled against the Scions of the Seventh Dawn, she was overtaken by fury and demanded that Lolorito be brought forth to face immediate judgment.

At this, Papashan shook his head. "I suggest you first allow Lord Lolorito to explain his motives, Your Grace," he said quietly. "Naught good ever comes of rushing to conclusions."

The following day, Nanamo summoned the foremost members of the Syndicate to the Fragrant Chamber—Lord Lolorito Nanarito, the purported mastermind of recent events; Flame General Raubahn Aldynn; and Dewlala Dewla, head of the Order of Nald'thal. Thus were the Monetarist, Royalist, and neutral factions each represented.

"I take it this intimate little meeting was intended as an opportunity for me to explain my actions," Lolorito declared airily.

"If there is aught you would say, then say it now," Nanamo responded with as much calm as she could muster.

"Very well," he sighed, as if indulging a spoiled child, and paused for a moment to remove his mask. It was considered a sign of great disrespect to wear such accoutrements to an audience with the sultana, but the Monetarist had always excused his discourtesy with the claim that his eyes were sensitive to bright light. Now, however, he stood barefaced without the slightest hint of discomfort.

"Forgive my candor, Your Grace, but it has become painfully obvious that you underestimate the dangers facing our great nation." The elder Lalafell's golden-eyed gaze remained steady upon the sultana's face while he delivered his blunt appraisal.

Raubahn's jaw clenched visibly, but he bowed his head and said nothing. Noting the Flame General's struggle from the corner of her eye, Nanamo motioned for the merchant to continue. She would heed Papashan's advice, and listen to Lolorito's account in its entirety— though she could gladly have strangled the preening little swine.

Somewhat predictably, Lolorito had come prepared to make his case. He spoke at length on the threat posed by the new emperor and a united Garlemald, warning that it was only a matter of time before the Garleans resumed their Eorzean campaign. To destabilize Ul'dah's government at such a juncture, he contended, was reckless in the extreme.

"To prevent Your Grace from enacting such a…*radical* reform, Teledji Adeledji chose the simple expedient of assassination. I merely slipped the reins of this foul scheme from his fumbling hands."

Nanamo caught herself clenching her fists as the merchant calmly explained how it had been necessary to maintain the illusion of her death in order to expose Teledji's sympathizers and thereby uproot the villain's widespread corruption. *The audacity of the man…*

"Had you deigned to consult with the Syndicate on the matter of your abdication, then perhaps such extreme measures could have been avoided," Lolorito smirked. "At the very least, Your Grace might have sought the advice of the General before making such a momentous and far-reaching decision."

Nanamo stiffened, each word a dagger in her breast. Lolorito was quite right. She had deliberately concealed her plans from Raubahn, knowing he would attempt to dissuade her from her course.

All she had wanted was a government answerable to the people—a government able to set aside self-interest and devote the nation's resources to solving Ul'dah's many problems, not least the ever-worsening refugee crisis. She had harbored hopes that the General, supported by a populace that had loved him since his days as a Coliseum champion, would continue to play a leading role in her imagined republic. Naturally, Lolorito and his fellow merchant princes would purchase influence as they always had, but the prospect of their wealth lining the pockets of the common man had seemed to her an acceptable trade.

But what tragedy has come of my clumsy maneuvering? The ensuing chaos had cost her dearest friend his arm, and all but destroyed the Scions of the Seventh Dawn, an organization to which she and every other Eorzean owed so much. A wave of regret rose up within her, and for a moment she felt she might drown in her sorrow.

"Of course, the execution of my plan was not without its flaws," Lolorito continued in an even, unhurried tone. "I did not anticipate the escape of the Scions, nor the violence that followed their flight from the palace—a most unwelcome complication."

According to Lolorito, accusing the Warrior of Light of murder and implicating the Scions as accomplices had been Teledji's idea. He speculated that the late Syndicate member wished to "repay" the Archons for interfering in the passing of the Carteneau Reclamation Bill. Lolorito himself purported to bear no ill will towards the order, but was forced to play along with their capture so that Teledji would remain ignorant of Ilberd's duplicity. Once the charade had ended, he assured Nanamo, he had fully intended to clear the false charges and release the Antecedent and her companions.

Nanamo railed inwardly at the implication that, by refusing to accept wrongful imprisonment, the Scions had brought retribution upon themselves. With an effort she hoped did not show upon her features, she held her breath and counted to ten.

"Regrettably, I did not anticipate the extent of Ilberd's insubordination," the merchant went on, oblivious to Nanamo's rising ire. "You are aware of our...disagreement with regard to the General's treatment, I believe?"

The sultana nodded mechanically, and replied after a moment, "I cannot well imagine why Captain Ilberd should desire General Aldynn's death."

Lolorito nodded in turn, and launched into another practiced explanation. He had, he revealed, initially secured Ilberd's services with the promise of sufficient weaponry and funding to transform Ala Mhigo's refugees into a well-armed and well-trained militia. These "resistance fighters" were to be deployed to their former homeland, where they would hinder the advance of imperial forces.

"As well as delaying the Garlean invasion, this mobilization would have had the added advantage of thinning the throng of refugees crowding Ul'dah's walls," the merchant pronounced with no small satisfaction, the beginnings of a smile tugging at the corner of his mouth.

At a look from the brooding Raubahn, the smile vanished, but Lolorito pressed on, "Alas, General, your mere existence presented Ilberd with something of a problem."

The Monetarist likened the former gladiator's position in the Syndicate to a beacon of hope for Ala Mhigo's displaced and downtrodden. Many, he noted with faint amusement, preferred to cast their gaze towards the light of an unattainable star, rather than turn and face the grim shadows of their troubled reality.

"Ilberd believed that the General's death was the only cure for this pernicious romanticism," the merchant continued, turning back to the sultana. "But while there may have been some truth to that, we needed our one-armed friend alive if we were to persuade Your Grace to sit the throne once more. And therein lay the root of our contention."

Had Raubahn been executed...what then? Would I have thrown reason to the desert winds, and called once more for the sultanate's dissolution? Nanamo suspected that she would. *Damn you, Lolorito.*

"Pray accept this token, Your Grace. Mayhap this *material* example of my support will remove any lingering doubts as to my loyalties..."

Nanamo accepted a scroll from the merchant's outstretched hand, and unfurled the fine vellum sheet. She read aloud the contents of the document—a legal contract that, when signed, would confer ownership of all of Teledji Adeledji's assets, and half of Lolorito's personal wealth, to the crown.

"Seven hells!" Raubahn roared, his patience finally spent. "You think to bury your sins under a mountain a coin?!"

A single gesture from the sultana was enough to silence him. He set his jaw, still scowling, while Lolorito affected a wounded air.

"My dear General, is not the sacrifice of coin the most fitting means for a merchant to express his contrition? You will note that there are no stipulations or constraints on how Her Grace might spend this fortune. Build a monument to the Scions, ease the suffering of the refugees—the possibilities are endless," Lolorito beamed benignly. "I would humbly suggest, however, that *some* thought be spared for the looming imperial invasion."

Having dispensed this final pearl of wisdom, the merchant addressed the sultana once more. "I thank you for your patient audience, Your Grace. Now, if you will excuse me, there are pressing matters to which I must attend."

With that, Lolorito replaced his mask and, without waiting for the sultana's leave to withdraw, strode briskly from the chamber.

And so the meeting ended.

Drained, Nanamo retired to her private quarters to reflect on the merchant's words. *I cannot forgive the man his methods*, she mused, *but mine own scheme is no less deserving of censure.* Her shortsighted resolve had invited bloodshed and turmoil, and she knew not how she might atone for her wrongdoing. For his part, Lolorito had surrendered a princely share of his riches—which, as a merchant, was an act akin to relinquishing his own flesh and blood. But what could she, as sultana, do to repay the debt she had accrued?

"Fetch General Aldynn!"

Raubahn arrived at her chambers soon after, escorted by Nanamo's new lady-in-waiting, and she handed him the contract without a word. When the General saw the sultana's flowing signature appended to the document, his brow knit in consternation.

"I despise that man," she declared, flatly.

"As do I," came the reply.

"And yet, I despise myself even more. I failed to confide in my most trusted advisor and blithely invited open rebellion within the Syndicate. My callow ambition has visited pain and suffering upon those who deserve it least, and shown me to be the greatest fool of all!"

At this, Raubahn could only bow his head.

"Lolorito is a callous, calculating villain, driven only by greed," Nanamo grated. "But in spite of this, I cannot ignore his skill as a politician nor the deeds he has performed in service to Ul'dah."

Nanamo closed her eyes as warring emotions threatened to engulf her once more. But she held firm to her emerging purpose, and looked up to find Raubahn gazing upon her with fatherly concern.

"Summon the war council, General," she commanded in a clear, strong voice. "We must discuss how Ishgard may be reintegrated into the Eorzean Alliance. And then we shall explore our strategy for opposing the inevitable advance of the Empire."

Nanamo took a deep breath, and fixed Raubahn with a resolute stare. "I will be intimidated by Lolorito and his ilk no longer. No matter her personal feelings, a sultana must make use of every resource at her disposal...for coin and country."

She had ascended the throne at the age of five and sworn an oath at her coronation—empty words that she had memorized but not understood. The oath she swore now, however—though it better befitted a soldier than a sultana—resonated through her entire being.

"For coin and country," Raubahn echoed in his deep rumble.

Then the one-armed general smiled, and Nanamo could not help but do the same.

Ul'dah was a sultanate once more.

Tales from the Calm

A Malm in Her Shoes

Leveilleur. Alisaie took immense pride in her name. It served as a constant reminder to the world of her connection to her grandsire, the great Louisoix Leveilleur—the man who spared the realm of Eorzea from the worst ravages of the Seventh Umbral Calamity. Needless to say, such noble heritage came with certain expectations, and she had worked tirelessly at the Studium to surpass them. Despite her many laudable academic achievements, however, Alisaie's tomboyish behavior and sharp tongue—honed through years spent bickering with her equally gifted twin brother—had earned her the scorn of her peers. But Alisaie took solace in the thought that Louisoix had himself been possessed of a mischievous streak, and had never been one to suffer fools gladly.

Having completed her schooling, Alisaie had traveled to Eorzea in a fever of expectation, eager to see the realm for which her grandsire had sacrificed so much. But what she found there was not at all as she had imagined. And so, after much soul-searching, she had resolved to explore the land in search of a cause for which to fight—a purpose of her own. She would travel alone, accompanied by neither servants nor adventurers—and *certainly* not by her brother—adamant that the impressions she formed be unsullied by the opinions of others.

And now, after many days on the road, she found herself in the barren lands of Thanalan. Having toiled for malms in the relentless midday heat, she relented and sought refuge in a wayside tavern.

"Stubborn bitch!"

She squinted towards the source of the outburst, her eyes not yet adjusted to the dim interior, and made out a burly man towering over a young lady. The girl—a traveler, judging by her attire—stood undaunted, even as the brute raised a meaty fist.

Alisaie sighed. She had grown weary of these barbaric people and their childish squabbles, but had not forgotten her grandfather's old admonishment: *"To ignore the plight of those one might conceivably save is not wisdom—it is indolence."*

"It is far too hot for fighting," Alisaie announced loudly. "But if you insist on hitting something, then I would be happy to arrange a meeting between you and the floor."

Both quarrelers flinched at the sound of Alisaie's voice, turning to meet her cold gaze with almost identical expressions of stunned surprise.

And thus did Alisaie make the acquaintance of young Emery, the traveling merchant.

According to Emery, her caravan was ordinarily accompanied by a guard, but after said sellsword had unexpectedly refused the offer of a new contract, she had been left at the mercy of a customer who thought to intimidate her into accepting a less than favorable trade. Having witnessed how effortlessly Alisaie cowed the man, however, the merchant now seemed determined to convince her savior to serve as the caravan's new escort.

Like all roving peddlers, Emery explained, her associates made their living trading goods between far-flung settlements. *But*, she claimed, the traders of her particular caravan knew all the shortest routes, and were famed for the swiftness with which they brought new wares to market. In short, one could wish for no finer employers.

Despite the nakedness of Emery's patter, Alisaie found that she was enthralled. Every aspect of the merchant's nomadic lifestyle seemed unspeakably fascinating. Though she took pains to hide her enthusiasm, lest she seem ignorant of the world, the grin on the merchant's face suggested that Alisaie's attempt to feign disinterest was less than successful. And so, after pausing as if to weigh the decision, she agreed.

In the days that followed, Alisaie studied the merchants' ways, swiftly growing accustomed to their routine, such that when the caravan eventually pulled in to its next port of call—a village nestled at the base of the Sea of Spires—she felt like a changed woman. With new eyes, she appraised their destination. The settlement's central bazaar was meager compared to the sprawling markets of Ul'dah, but the steady stream of visitors who came and went lent the place a kind of bustling energy.

Though her duties had thus far asked little more of her than to clear obstinate flocks of aldgoats from the road, she breathed a sigh of relief as the wagons trundled safely into the village. *I shall never take caravan guards for granted again*, she vowed, feeling utterly drained by the demands of constant vigilance.

For a time, Alisaie simply stood and watched as the merchants hurried back and forth in a flurry of preparation. Her silent observations were soon interrupted, however, by the arrival of a breathless Emery.

"There's much and more to be done, Mistress Leveilleur," the young woman chirped. "We'll need your help with the selling."

"Selling? But I've no experience with—"

Seizing her hand, Emery dragged Alisaie towards the stalls her colleagues had erected in the village square. Residents and visitors alike were already crowding around the merchants, inspecting the wares that neatly lined the makeshift shelves.

Alisaie stopped short when she saw the swelling throng. *This is a task for my brother*, she thought with a twinge of panic. *If Alphinaud were here, he would already be striding into their midst, sporting that infernal grin of his.* Yet even as she attempted to back away, the merchant girl yanked her forward once more.

"You remember the talk we had about pricing, don't you?"

"Well, yes, but surely you do not expect me to—"

But Emery had already swiveled on her heels and begun serving a waiting customer, leaving Alisaie to talk to the breeze. She was still standing openmouthed behind the counter, entertaining thoughts of escape, when a matronly, middle-aged woman thrust a bolt of cloth towards her.

"How much for this, then?"

Alisaie stared blankly at the cloth, her mind in disarray. And then she glimpsed Emery's brief backwards glance, and the mischievous smile that played on her lips. *At least one of us is enjoying this.* The noise in the square rose as the haggling began in earnest, and Alisaie permitted herself a sigh.

After a hard day's bargaining, the caravan had sold much of its stock, and that evening the merchants retired to a dilapidated inn on the edge of the village proper. Exhausted, Alisaie sat down heavily on one of the two beds in her cramped room, and began flicking through the volume on arcane theory she had purchased during her stay in Ul'dah. Ever since her days as student, it had been a nightly ritual for her to open a book before bed and note down new findings in her journal. Should she discover any promising techniques, she would rise early the following morning and attempt to put her learning into practice.

But hours of unfamiliar work had taken their toll, and she was only a few lines into her current chapter when her eyelids began to droop. By the time Emery came in, she was all but asleep. The merchant girl stifled a laugh as Alisaie snatched reflexively at the tome that had begun to slide from her lap.

"Sorry for dragging you along today," Emery said, smiling. "I thought you might find it entertaining."

"'Twas certainly…an experience," Alisaie replied with a tired grin.

Emery sat down on the bed opposite, and glanced at Alisaie's book with interest.

"You never miss a day, do you," she said, shaking her head. "Trying to keep up with that brother of yours, eh?"

"Mayhap at first," Alisaie admitted. "But it was my grandfather who taught me the value of reading. And it is a habit that I am proud to have maintained."

"It is well that you respect your grandsire's teachings, Alisaie, but I doubt he meant for you to fall asleep sitting up," Emery chided gently.

With that, she took the still-open volume perched on Alisaie's knees, flipped the silk bookmark back into place, and snapped it shut.

"I hadn't finished…" Alisaie managed, even as the girl dropped the book onto the pile of her belongings.

Emery stretched and yawned.

"It will still be there on the morrow," she said, and then her impish grin returned. "And it's not as if you didn't learn a few things today—you made your first sale, for heavens' sakes! I'm certain both Nald'thal and your grandsire would forgive you for missing a single night of study."

Ordinarily, Alisaie would not countenance such convenient excuses, but the warmth of Emery's manner had disarmed her. There was a familiar kindness in her words that set Alisaie's heart at ease.

Both girls readied themselves for bed, and Emery illuminated the room with another of her radiant smiles before reaching out to extinguish the lamp.

"Sleep well."

And that was the last night Alisaie would spend in her young friend's company.

A sliver of sunlight fell across Alisaie's face, and she slowly opened her eyes. Pulling herself up to a sitting position, she spent a moment looking around before remembering where she was—in one of the private rooms of a Gridanian inn. The day had just dawned and she had been dreaming.

The journey she made with Emery had ended long ago, the vault of her mind the only place where she would ever see the girl again. On the day following Alisaie's debut as a merchant, the caravan had set off for its next destination during one of Thanalan's rare thunderstorms. The deluge made it hard to see, and still harder to steer, so the wagons were spaced out more than usual as they slipped and slid along a muddy path that cut through an otherwise impassable bluff.

A muffled rumble was the only warning they had before the cliff-sides collapsed. In the space of a heartbeat, the carriages bringing up the rear and all who rode aboard them were buried beneath a mountain of sodden earth. And Emery was gone.

As fate would have it, Alisaie had been riding on the lead wagon, and emerged from the ordeal without so much as a bruise. She duly carried out her contract, escorting the surviving merchants to the next town before bidding them farewell. Mind still numb with shock, she was some distance away when she chanced to glance back at the caravan and saw how few of the wagons remained. Her chest constricted with sudden grief, and the tears finally fell.

After that, Alisaie had returned to traveling alone, filing the memory of each new meeting and parting away inside her breast, and taking none into her confidence. It was in the lonely days that followed that she chanced to hear rumors of an unknown band of heroes that appeared to be doing the work of the Scions. And thus, at long last, she found a purpose. The gossip in the ports made much of the recent events in Ishgard, but she doggedly followed the underlying thread of primal activity. Alisaie would learn the nature of these champions whose course appeared destined to cross that of her brother and his comrades.

She swung her legs over the side of the bed, stretched, and threw open the shutters. As she gazed out at the morning sky, a fragment of her dream rose unbidden: the image of Emery's smiling face. Alisaie recalled the girl's well-meaning words with an aching sadness.

Some things do not last until the morrow.

A Display of Ingenuity

The winter of the Garlean Empire's thirty-eighth year was a bitterly cold one, and the capital lay muffled under a thick blanket of snow. Black uniform stark against the pristine white, a boy strode as briskly as he could through knee-high drifts, his boots spraying powdery flakes before him with every hurried step.

"And I'm the first to arrive!"

The boy huffed in satisfaction as he stood before the main entrance to the Magitek Academy's central library, having sprang up the stately stone steps two at a time. Brushing his silvery hair out of his eyes, however, his moment of triumph was cut short by the sight of a skinny youth, blond and smirking, sidling into view from behind a colossal marble pillar.

"Sorry to disappoint you, *Garlond*—but you'll have to get up earlier than that to beat me."

Such was the first meeting between Cid Garlond and Nero Scaeva—at least, as far as the young Cid was aware.

The pair were similarly exceptional.

As the son of Midas nan Garlond—the Empire's foremost authority on magitek—and a renowned child prodigy in his own right, Cid had been invited to apply to the Magitek Academy some few moons before. Nero, too, had earned fame as the genius of his province, and would have been comfortably the youngest student in the institution, were it not for the presence of the equally precocious Cid. Though both boys were barely into their twelfth summers, their extraordinary achievements had qualified them to sit the entrance examinations four years earlier than was normally permitted.

Accustomed to always being top of the class back home, Nero was not amused to find that the only other boy his age was held in higher esteem. His theretofore unsurpassed brilliance had secured him a patron and passage to the capital, and when he finally laid eyes upon his silver-haired rival during the Academy's entrance ceremony, he had vowed to outdo him in every conceivable manner.

"Do I know you?" Cid snapped in irritation. Gifted though he was, he was no less a twelve-year-old boy. And this brash youth who had addressed him with such scorn had immediately raised his hackles.

"You *should*. But I don't suppose you've any time for peasants from the provinces," Nero shot back. "The name's Scaeva. Nero Scaeva. I'm the one who's going to upstage you at the exhibition by taking home first prize."

The Imperial Youth Magitek Exhibition was a showcase for aspiring engineers from across the Empire to submit their magitek creations for expert appraisal. Cid had entered an invention a year before joining the Academy, going on to become the youngest ever participant to win the event's highest honor. And it was to research his submission for this year's contest that he had endeavored to arrive at the library just as it was due to open its doors for the day.

Cid knew that many of the older students regarded him as the person to beat, but none had gone so far as to declare their rivalry directly to his face. As such, Nero's cocksure challenge flustered him more than he cared to admit.

From that day onwards, Nero made a habit of antagonizing Cid at every opportunity.

If Cid should borrow a research volume, he would declare its content "elementary." If Cid was using the workshop's lathe to make a part, its quality would be "substandard." Even the selections Cid made at the lunch hall did not escape judgment, invariably befitting "the palate of an infant."

"Damn you, Nero," Cid fumed to himself as he worked to assemble the delicate pieces of his submission. "Will you never leave me be?"

And so the months passed.

Spring came at length, though the weather refused to acknowledge it, the snow showing no signs of melting as the capital shivered in winter's lingering chill. Yet despite the cold outside, the exhibition hall was stifling—the air heated by the frenzied activity of the many students within. Wearing variously panicked expressions, they bustled around their respective pieces, desperate to ensure a smooth performance for the contest's final and most heavily weighted category: the practical demonstration.

Cid himself was busy testing each component of the flying machine he had constructed, focusing intently upon the flapping motion of his invention's aether-infused wings.

"You don't honestly think a flimsy toy like that will impress the judges…?"

A voice dripping with disdain prodded at Cid's consciousness, shattering his concentration. *Agh, not now, Scaeva…*

"My hypercurrent cannon will garner ten times—nay, *a hundred* times—the interest!"

Nero had arrived cradling a sleek tube in his arms, which he now proudly presented for Cid's inspection. Though his soul cried out to tell him where to shove it, Cid's better self reasoned that he would gain nothing from rising to this obvious provocation, and he continued working on his own device in determined silence.

An instant later, a deafening roar reverberated around the auditorium.

"What in the—?!"

An explosion, offered his inner voice. Suppressing a smile, Cid stood up to see whose invention had met with misfortune. But rather than twisted pieces of magitek, his questing gaze picked out a group of soldiers emerging from a haze of drifting white smoke. They belonged to no legion. The mismatched equipment, the unshaven faces, the unkempt hair—it all pointed to one thing. *Rebels.*

The initial moment of shock was broken by a single, piercing scream, and then the hall dissolved into chaos. Students clambered over each other in their haste to flee, abandoning their precious works without so much as a backwards glance.

"Th-this is an outrage!" stammered Nero, the sight of armed dissidents sending cracks through his usual veneer of self-assurance. "How did this rabble slip into the capital?!"

Cid appeared stunned by the scene unfolding before him, but though his body was slow to respond, his mind was already assembling the puzzle of the who, the what, and the why.

As he watched, the apparent leader of the insurgent group quickly scanned the faces in the exhibition hall then turned to bark orders at his fellows. "The target's not here. You lot keep the imperials at bay—the rest of you, upstairs with me!" A handful of rebels then began erecting barricades and ejecting clumps of cowering students, while their comrades headed towards a nearby staircase.

"They're looking for someone…"

The moment Cid whispered the words out loud, he knew. Of all the dignitaries currently in attendance, the most notable was, without a doubt, the judging panel's chairman—the Empire's preeminent engineer, Midas nan Garlond.

Father! Though Cid had yet to ascertain the motive, it was enough to know his sire's life was in danger.

He clutched his flying machine close to his chest and ran. Avoiding the throng of panicked students scrambling towards the building's exits, he made for a staircase and raced up to the second floor. If he remembered correctly, a conference room had been set aside for the judges to take their ease during the exhibition's lengthy preparation periods.

Slowing from his mad dash, Cid crept along the last few yalms of a side corridor. From around the corner, he heard a man snarl.

"Call off the test or you die! I won't ask again!"

All the pieces fell into place. His father had scarce been at home this past moon, his time spent traveling back and forth between the capital and Bozja Citadel in the frontier lands, where some important—and confidential—experiment was taking place at the behest of the Emperor himself. And the garb of these rebels seemed to match the descriptions he had read of that province's people.

Their plan was obvious now: by taking his sire prisoner, they hoped to put a stop to whatever it was he was working on, imagining his experiment a threat to their home. The military would be reluctant to endanger the "Father of Magitek," and thus they need not fear any heavily armed reprisals—in the short term, at least…

"After *Daddy*, are they?"

Cid jolted in surprise, almost dropping his flying machine. Turning his head, he saw a blond boy crouched behind him, also hugging his invention.

"Keep your bloody voice down, Nero!" Cid hissed. "Why in the seven hells did you follow me?!"

121

"I couldn't let you run off and get killed," Nero explained with forced nonchalance. "You wouldn't be there to see me win the contest."

"The *contest*?!" Cid spat, barely stifling a shout. "Is that all you can think about?!"

"Only until I've won it," came the reply. "And while I am certain my cannon will take first prize, it will be a hollow victory without your submission sitting there below it on the podium."

Incensed, Cid closed his eyes and took a deep breath—but in that moment, an idea came to him. His eyes snapped open, and flicked between the magitek devices they both still held in viselike grips.

"If you're so keen to have our entries judged," he whispered, fixing Nero with a stare, "help me save the judges."

Thus began an unprecedented collaboration between the two young prodigies. Concealing themselves within a sanitation closet, they proceeded to strip down the hypercurrent cannon and attach it to the flying machine, all without a word of disagreement passing their lips. The result was a rudimentary combat drone.

"We've created an airborne magitek turret!" Nero crowed in delight.

Ignoring his companion's enthusiasm, Cid fiddled with his half of the control module they had pieced together from the leftover parts. The compact ceruleum engine snorted comically as it whirred to life, but despite the additional weight, the newly built turret lifted smoothly off the floor, its aetherwings beating slow and steady.

"Right." Cid looked up, satisfied that the device was operational. "I'll do the flying; you do the firing."

"As you command, *Master Garlond*."

Nero threw wide the closet door, and Cid sent the drone hurtling down the hallway at maximum speed. Once around the corner, a crackling burst from the cannon struck the rebel standing guard. His limbs twitched spasmodically as he fell senseless to the floor. Without slowing, the buzzing machine barreled on into the conference room, its breathless operators a few steps behind.

"It's the army!"

The Bozjans scrambled to bring their weapons to bear, their leader stepping forward to answer the sudden intrusion. "Stop right there!" he demanded. "We have a hosta—" And there his words devolved into an agonized scream as a bolt of energy struck him squarely in the chest.

"Enjoy the demonstration!"

Nero jabbed at the firing button with fiendish glee, and arcs of crackling lightning filled the room.

A short while later, the imperial guard arrived at the auditorium. The Emperor's finest duly cut through the defenders downstairs and stormed the upper floor, only to be greeted by the sight of a heap of unconscious insurgents…and a glassy-eyed Midas nan Garlond—all victims of Nero's indiscriminate display.

Once every trace of the incident had been swept away, and the affected parties afforded sufficient time to recover, the interrupted exhibition held its awards ceremony. The identity of the winner came as no surprise to anyone. Or rather, the winners. First prize was awarded to Cid Garlond and Nero Scaeva, in honor of their jointly created magitek turret.

"Something troubling you, Chief?"

Cid's head snapped up at Jessie's query, leaving his hand with no beard to stroke.

"Oh… No. I was just…thinking about the old days."

Jessie raised an eyebrow. "Anything to do with that data you requested?"

It was true that, ever since he had asked for a certain research file to be smuggled out of the Empire, Cid had perhaps indulged in more brooding than was healthy. He had work to do, he knew, and the stakes could hardly be higher.

"Worried about me?" he teased, forcing a smile. "I'm fine, Jessie. I've made peace with the past. Besides…" he continued, the grin genuine now, "the memories aren't *all* bad."

The time for deliberation was over. Nodding to his colleagues, Cid Garlond, master engineer, strode off to join his companions in their fated and final confrontation.

The Hunt Begins

One might think it a blessing to be born into the ruling family of a vast and powerful empire, but for the young Prince Zenos—great-grandson of Solus zos Galvus, revered founding father of the Garlean Empire—it was a curse.

From the beginning, Zenos was alone. His lady mother succumbed to illness shortly after bringing him into the world, and his lord father was seldom present, occupied as he was with his military campaigns and political maneuvering. And while the prince was surrounded by count-less servants, they were as machina to him, trundling about on invisible rails, bereft of independent thought. Nor did he hold the learned men and women who served as his tutors in much higher regard. His brilliant mind found their lessons—their very existence—monotonous, and he preferred the silent company of books.

With such an upbringing, he could not choose but be different from other children. Indeed, it could be said that he was never a child at all. Innocence and playfulness were quite alien to him, the former expunged by his earliest schooling and the latter afforded no outlet. His days were uniformly joyless, and he went about his scheduled tasks with apathy. Thus did he pass his first four and ten summers—in a steel-grey blur of tedium.

"Arm yourself," the stranger ordered without preamble.

Today, as per routine, Zenos had come to the training hall for his martial drills—a crucial part of any future emperor's education. But this time, he found not his usual tutor waiting for him, but an unfamiliar figure. The man's skin, baked copper by the sun, was an uncommon sight in the frozen climes of the imperial capital, and he was small of stature, if sinuously muscled. Most telling of all, however, was the absence of a third eye upon his forehead. This man was not Garlean, but a native of one of the provinces.

And there, Zenos lost what little interest he had in the foreigner. Having assessed his appearance, the spark of curiosity promptly faded from the prince's eyes.

Wearily, Zenos nodded. *A different tutor*, he thought, *for the selfsame lesson.* Hours of being reminded to grip his sword correctly, of being told to stand this way and that. Combat training was as numbingly dull as academic studies, but he had not the will to refuse anymore, if indeed he ever had. Zenos reached out and grasped a practice sword from the rack...and found the hall's cold floor pressed against his face.

What in the world...? He instinctively tried to regain his feet, but the floor shifted beneath him and he fell back down. The pain in the back of his skull told him that he had been struck, though he neither saw nor heard his assailant's approach.

"You are dead," the foreigner said as he stood over Zenos, his voice betraying no emotion. He spun on his heels and strode off.

"Wait... We haven't even started..." Zenos muttered groggily as he tried again in vain to clamber to his feet. His tutor did not spare him a backward glance.

"The dead do not learn. They sleep."

That encounter marked a change in Zenos's routine. Whereas before, martial drills took place thrice weekly and never on consecutive days, the very next day he was summoned to the training hall once more.

"Arm yourself."

The same words uttered in the same tone. This time Zenos knew better than to take his eyes off his nameless tutor. He crept over to the weapons rack, snatched up his blade, and raised it hurriedly in a defensive stance.

For all the good it did. Though he was certain he was beyond striking range, he was taken square in the chest and sent sprawling. As before, he caught not a glimpse of his opponent's blade. And thus did the drills continue all week, ending before they had even begun.

Save in the fleeting company of his lord father, this was, as far as Zenos could recall, the first time he had found himself in a situation beyond his control. Even had his tutors not treated him with deference, Zenos had always had the better of them, regularly surprising them with brilliance. It could scarcely have been more different with this foreigner. He accorded Zenos not a shred of respect, and if he was trying to teach, he gave no indication of it. All he seemed interested in doing was demonstrating the peerlessness of his own swordsmanship.

The tenth day saw Zenos limping back to his chambers, cradling a throbbing shoulder, when his father's voice rang out behind him.

"How goes your training?"

As if you don't know. Though his clothing did a good job of hiding the countless welts and bruises now covering his body, Varis would have received the reports from his son's servants. He knew full well about these daily thrashings, and had permitted them to continue.

"Very well, Father," Zenos replied, smiling.

It was a twisted trial for a father to impose upon his son, yet Zenos felt neither indignation nor humiliation. Whatever his father's true intent, he regarded the adversity as a gift. Up until this point in his life, he had faced no challenge worthy of the name, and the one that his newest tutor presented instilled him with a burning sense of purpose—a reason to rise each morning rooted not in duty but desire.

Without further word, Varis nodded and left Zenos as he found him, so ending their first encounter in moons.

Two painful and invigorating weeks passed. While Zenos was still unable to swing his blade in reply to his opponent, he could now make out the arcs of his blows. And long after his tutor had taken his leave, he could be seen training alone each day, honing skills and tempering flesh. *But skill and strength are not enough*, Zenos realized. *I require knowledge.* And so he took to scouring tomes in the royal library in a bid to identify the techniques being employed against him.

At length, he found his answer within conquest records written by a pilus prior. The style, it transpired, was called the Unyielding Blade, and it hailed from the region of Corvos in southern Ilsabard. Now armed with a name, Zenos set out next to find treatises on the subject, but instructional resources proved elusive and his search yielded no fruit. If anything, however, this only added to the thrill of the hunt. *So be it. If the techniques cannot be had through text, I shall acquire them through practice.*

The following week, Zenos made it his mission to observe his opponent's every movement, even if it meant leaving himself open to a good beating. From his footwork to his stance to his strokes, he drank it all in as a thirsty man drains his cup. And by the time a moon had passed, he found he could turn away some few strikes before succumbing to the onslaught.

"Arm yourself," he ordered as Zenos took his place. The boy had improved in recent days, he had to concede, but there were limits that he could never overcome. *Even* with *a willing teacher*, he added inwardly. Today would doubtless bring more of the same. He watched as his charge reached out and grasped a practice sword from the rack...and slashed at him without warning.

The boy was a good ten paces away. Short of throwing his sword, he could not hope to reach him. Yet an instant later, he found himself scrambling to dodge the energy wave that hurtled narrowly past his side.

"You— How did you do that?"

He could not hide his shock at having his own technique used against him. For the Unyielding Blade was passed down only from master to pupil, and he was the last remaining soul to bear the title of swordmaster. A native of subjugated Corvos, he and his fellow practitioners had risen up against their imperial oppressors, but for all their skill at arms, they had found themselves hopelessly outnumbered. The forces led by Varis crushed their rebellion and slew all of its members, but for good or ill, he alone had been spared their fate, and clapped in irons instead. On Varis's orders, he had then been brought to the imperial capital specifically to train Zenos while his family was taken hostage to guarantee his obedience. Their faces flashed before his eyes, only to disappear when the boy cleared his throat.

What Zenos had done defied all reason. Even had there been some other swordmaster to impart the Unyielding Blade's secrets to him, he should not have been be able to employ the technique. For the style required the practitioner to imbue his weapon with his own aether, an ability famously beyond the reach of trueborn Garleans. Yet here was a trueborn Garlean—and a stripling at that—who had mastered the technique in less than a moon. It was impossible. Unthinkable. *Unforgivable.*

"You seem surprised," Zenos replied flatly. "Why?"

The room seemed to turn red. "Do not insult me, boy," he managed, his voice trembling slightly. "Ours is a proud art with a thousand-year history!"

The remark had cut him to the quick, slicing through the façade of indifference he had attempted to maintain. Initiating an impudent prince into his style had never been his intent. Nay, he had come to the imperial palace intent upon assassinating the boy's father, Varis, even if it meant sacrificing his wife and daughter. No price was too high to avenge his fallen comrades. *The gods will forgive me*, he had told himself more than once.

But now, he decided to cast aside all of his carefully laid plans, all his patiently bided time, and slay the boy who stood before him. He would not suffer a Garlean—least of all the issue of his loathed foe—to steal the techniques his forebears had spent generations perfecting. He could not conceive of a greater dishonor to their legacy.

"The Unyielding Blade is not for the likes of you to wield!"

Even with blunted practice swords, masters of the style can empower their weapons with aether to kill with ease. And so he charged at Zenos, hatred contorting his features. But instead of flinching, the boy scoffed in disdain, and he felt a flash of annoyance.

He had expected to finish it quickly. With each strike that failed to find its mark, however, his confidence waned. Zenos was an impenetrable wall of ice, nullifying his onslaught of energy waves with his own while scarcely seeming to move. He had stayed his blade for but a heartbeat to consider his next move when Zenos lunged at him.

The slashes came at him from everywhere and nowhere, as a pack of hounds snapping at prey in the dark, and it was all he could do to fend them off. The boy's movements seemed random, yet there was a method to the madness, one to which he had no answer. Ere long, he found himself backed into a corner, the grip of his sword slick with sweat. So thoroughly overwhelmed, he was forced to admit that Zenos was no pampered prince to be scorned, but a true warrior to be feared. But he would not—could not—admit defeat.

"No..." he whispered through gritted teeth. "Not to you... Not today..."

With a savage roar, he threw himself at Zenos, bringing his weapon down with every fiber of his being, willing it to strike home. The blade sang as it traced a vicious arc through the air…and fell from limp fingers to the floor with a clang. He looked down to see his lifeblood blossoming upon his chest, dripping from Zenos's hands, still gripping the sword hilt.

"The dead do not learn. They sleep. Is that not so?"

Zenos whispered by the Corvosi's ear, but his only response was to collapse to the ground, the sword still lodged in his breast, eyes open but unseeing. Zenos bared a bloodied hand to his slain foe. There, embedded in the cup of his palm, glinted a crystal fragment.

"*I* have learned two things, however. First, the inability to manipulate aether is a vexing disadvantage, and one which must be addressed."

Without so much as a blink, Zenos plucked the crystal free of his flesh, his own blood oozing from the open wound. He had buried it in his palm in a bid to force his body to release aether. And the risks had been great; in the worst case, his body's aetherial balance could have been altered irreversibly, even fatally. Yet in full knowledge of the dangers, naught else would suffice but to sate his curiosity and put this new fighting style to the proof.

Zenos continued. "Second, battle offers no euphoria, despite what the tales may claim. Deep down I had always known this, yet I find myself disappointed nonetheless."

He tossed the crystal at his opponent's corpse.

"Your payment for these two lessons."

So it was that Zenos yae Galvus's first true battle came to an end. Without further ceremony, he quit the training hall, washed, and put on fresh clothes. By the time he sat at table for his evening repast, he had quite forgotten the face of his tutor. And as he settled into bed, he prayed as earnestly as a boy of his years might that one day he would cross paths with a *worthy* foe and feel such exhilaration as the heroic epics promised. And then, with a sigh, he closed his eyes and knew the soundest sleep he had ever known.

Tales from the Storm

With Ishgard restored to the Eorzean Alliance, the bonds between the great nations were stronger than ever. Alas, this brief interlude of peace was brought to an end when the Griffin and his followers mounted an attack on Baelsar's Wall, drawing the Alliance and Garlemald into open war once more.

So it was that the Warrior of Light and his comrades joined forces with the Ala Mhigan Resistance, as well as the Doman Liberation Front in the Far East, and together launched a bold campaign to liberate two provinces from imperial rule. Though thousands of malms apart, the peoples of these two lands came together in common purpose against their oppressors, and took up arms to reclaim their freedom and dignity.

In Darkness Blooms the Lily

Ensconced in the private room of a tavern, a courtesan poured a cup of wine for a gentleman with practiced grace.

Tedious wretch, Yotsuyu cursed inwardly, betraying no hint of irritation. She had thought this simple man of war would be less resistant to her charms.

Over the course of an evening, she would use drink and desire to erode her mark's defenses, drawing out secrets one by one, before serving the most delicious morsels to her employer. As an imperial spy, it was an act she had performed a hundred times, and this night was meant to be no different.

But her guest was not cooperating. Zenos yae Galvus, legatus of the XIIth Imperial Legion, was clearly disinclined to trust his hosts from the Doman garrison. Despite the warmth of the sitting room, he made no move to shed his armor, receiving his cup with a gauntleted hand. His eyes were dull and focused on nothing, and yet in their depths she discerned a muted glimmer of anticipation. *What are you waiting for...?*

Originally, Yotsuyu's masters had assigned her a different mission. Lord Kaien, Doma's former ruler, was reported to have assembled an army, and it seemed an uprising was imminent.

Thus had she been tasked with infiltrating the ranks of the rebellion. She was to offer them military intelligence supposedly gleaned from imperial visitors to her establishment, and play the part of a devoted patriot, willing to risk her life to gather vital information. Once in place, she would instead funnel the rebel army's plans back to the Empire. A betrayal of her kith and kin, to be sure, though the courtesan felt not the slightest shred of remorse.

Was it not her closest kin—her foster parents and her late husband— who had made her life a living hell? And none who witnessed this treatment had lifted a finger in her defense. As far as Yotsuyu was concerned, her countrymen were complicit in her abuse, and deserving of the same punishment as her abusers.

Yet on the day she was to begin the operation, the garrison's intelligence officer called her back. They had received word that an imperial legatus would shortly be arriving from the capital to assess the situation in Doma. Lord Zenos was his name—one she had heard before.

With Emperor Solus on his deathbed, a clandestine war of succession was already being waged in Garlemald. Solus's eldest being dead, his grandson Varis was next in line to the throne, but the Emperor's second son Titus had other ideas, and no shortage of support. What he did not have, however, was Varis's standing with the military, nor less a ready heir—this Zenos.

As a public ally of Titus, the viceroy plainly considered the legatus a threat, Yotsuyu saw. And the fact that they would entrust her with so important a target bespoke how high she had risen in their esteem. *Finally, some recognition.* She favored the intelligence offer with a wintry smile.

"I understand Kaien and his fledgling rebellion have yet to be stamped out. Could it be that the viceroy's superiors are *unsatisfied* with this lack of progress?" Yotsuyu feigned a look of sympathy. "How galling it must be to have a political rival travel all this way just to prod one's sorest spots."

The officer frowned in consternation.

"We are well aware that Doma's present troubles afford our opponents an opportunity to undermine our position. But this visit also affords *us* an opportunity," he continued, fixing Yotsuyu with a meaningful stare. "If we were to tease from Zenos some insight into his father's plans, we may yet emerge from this exchange with the upper hand."

"It's all the same to me," Yotsuyu purred. "Another man, another evening. He passes the night in bliss, and I steal every word that falls from his careless tongue. Simple."

They had treated her like cattle, but now she held the switch. She had no taste for the sweet nothings men showered upon her—it was the spectacle of their graceless slide into self-destruction that sated her vengeful appetite. At least for a time.

Yet the plans of both Yotsuyu and the viceroy were defeated at the outset by Zenos's unshakable lassitude. The visiting legatus barely spared his host a glance as he lounged with obvious boredom on the cushions provided. Having braced himself for a humiliating examination of his failures, the viceroy withdrew in some confusion, leaving Yotsuyu to attend to the needs of his "guest."

The hour grew late, and Zenos emptied his cup again and again. But the wine may as well have been water for all the effect it seemed to have upon him.

Will the man never get drunk? Yotsuyu wondered in exasperation. Then, just as she had begun to contemplate simply throwing herself naked into his lap, he spoke.

"What manner of place is this…Doma?"

The courtesan hesitated at the sudden question. She had no shortage of answers, of course, and could gladly wax lyrical upon the shortcomings of her despised birthplace until dawn. But her task was to unburden her target of his secrets, not unburden herself. *At least he's talking. I'll loosen that tongue yet…* As she looked up, however, the perfunctory response she had prepared died in her throat. The eyes which had spent the evening staring past her now bored into the depths of her soul.

"I am weary of empty chatter," he warned. "Tell me instead how such a face came to hide such bitterness. The tale may serve to amuse me."

"Such a blunt manner you have, my lord," Yotsuyu quipped, unwilling to relinquish her façade. "Shall we blame the wine for this breach of etiquette?"

Zenos merely stared in silence. It was plain he had no intention of acknowledging her deflection. Rather than feel discomfited, however, Yotsuyu found herself spellbound, the glare of his undivided attention captivating in its brilliance. In an instant of clarity, she understood. *This man will go far.*

The sound of falling rain seeped into her consciousness, a sudden hammering downpour that dissolved the moment which had held her frozen. But a connection had been made.

"The briefest stay in Doma will tell you all you need to know, my lord," Yotsuyu began, "Yanxia is a dunghill."

Zenos drained the rest of his cup, and leaned forward with interest.

"Ah, *there you are*. It intrigues me to see a woman struggle with such rage, when tradition dictates that she appear meek."

"Tradition?" the courtesan spat. "My countrymen strangle themselves with the shackles of worn-out customs and formalities. Their eyes bulge and their limbs spasm, and *still* they cling to precious notions of honor and sacrifice."

Now that she had given voice to her hatred, the words came spilling forth unbidden. A deluge which would have continued unabated had Zenos not risen to his feet.

His eyes seemed to seek something beyond the walls of the tavern.

"Waiting on the storm to cover their approach…" he murmured. "I was curious to hear more of your story, but the evening's true entertainment has arrived."

"What—" Yotsuyu had barely uttered the question when the nearby window exploded inwards. Ears ringing from the noise, she registered several black-clad forms clambering in through the breach.

The intruders drew blades, and surrounded Zenos with appalling swiftness. Yotsuyu, meanwhile, scrambled backwards in a crouch, and took in the unfolding scene. *Assassins*, she realized coldly, *and not terribly discreet ones.* They had dressed themselves in the garb of shinobi, but their swords, and the manner in which they held them, were distinctly imperial.

"Bastards!" she screamed, furious at her own gullibility. *They sent me here to die!*

Not one of the masked killers so much as glanced in her direction. Zenos himself seemed unconcerned, bored even, as he surveyed the naked steel arrayed against him. Making no move to retrieve his own sword, propped out of reach against the wall, the legatus calmly addressed the room.

"'Lord Zenos, slain in the arms of a Doman courtesan.' Yes, such a scandal is worth the ignominy of failing to protect a royal guest." His lips curled into a humorless smile. "And should Doma's fugitive ruler be implicated in the plot, all the better. The viceroy would have his reinforcements within a week."

The assassins remained mute as they edged closer and closer. In the next instant they were upon him, blades flashing in synchrony, their tightening circle obscuring his armored form from Yotsuyu's view.

Bracing for the inevitable, she was momentarily confused when each of the attackers seemed to pause in unison, before slumping lifeless to the floor. As they fell, Zenos appeared to her to rise from the tangle of black-clad limbs like a vengeful angel... But in truth he stood motionless, his expression unchanged. In one hand he held an assassin's sword. *How...?* Yotsuyu gaped in disbelief, trying to make sense of what she had just witnessed. She could but assume that he had seized a blade at the last moment, and felled the entire band with one impossible cut.

"I had hoped that a land on the brink of rebellion might offer some measure of sport." The legatus looked down at his fallen opponents, and grunted in annoyance. "But if the viceroy imagines a handful of hired knives sufficient to remove me from the hunt, I have sorely overestimated my prey..."

Yotsuyu felt something warm trickle down her cheek. Unthinking, she raised a hand to wipe it away and was bemused to find her fingers stained red. Glancing down at her kimono, she saw that it was spattered with blood.

"Why do you smile?"

Looking up, she noticed the legatus gazing upon her once more, and realized that she was indeed smiling. Of the many imperial officers she had encountered, some reputed "great men," not one seemed so assured of his own power, nor so uninterested in projecting it.

Should this strength be brought to bear upon Doma, her wretched nation would finally meet the end it deserved. Zenos's eyes narrowed at her widening grin, and he strode uncaring over the bodies of the slain to bring his lips close to her blood-streaked face.

"What is your name?" he breathed, voice scarcely above a whisper.

When morning came, no mention of the failed assassination attempt was made, and Yotsuyu duly returned to her mission to infiltrate the rebel forces.

Days turned into weeks, and when the heady rush of that blood-soaked evening had at last begun to fade, Kaien staged his long-planned rebellion. Predictably, the Doman viceroy could not contain the revolt, and the XIIth Legion was dispatched to intervene. After sweeping through Yanxia, Zenos defeated Kaien himself in single combat, and the rebellion crumbled soon after.

Among the crowd of haggard onlookers "encouraged" to watch the XIIth Legion's subsequent victory parade through the enclave, a courtesan stood unregarded. She had eyes only for the man who marched at the head of the procession, his features blank and unchanging under the bitter scrutiny of the Doman citizenry. And when she slipped away to follow behind the soldiers, there were none who noted her absence.

Some few days later, the acting viceroy who would rule over the lands of Doma in Zenos's stead was announced: a woman by the name of Yotsuyu.

The power was hers now, to taunt, torment, and torture every miserable soul who huddled in her hated domain. Draped in an elegant kimono and twirling a slender pipe, she looked down from the walls of Doma Castle…and smiled.

O Nhaama, Where Art Thou

"Ours is the soil. Come, come—come and listen to my tale. A tale of a brother most radiant—"

At this, the young men gathered around the fire chuckled.

"Most radiant indeed! But like all great tales, it began long, long ago—at the beginning, with a father, a mother, a Steppe, and a people…"

From the forbidding heights of the Tail Mountains flow many khaal that wind their way to Azim Khaat. And upon this khaat rests a great stone monument. A sacred fortress forged by the Dawn Father himself. A throne upon which his children might bask in the sun.

In its shadow lived a proud, strong people. They who were descended from Azim, they who were destined to rule. The Oronir.

And among the Oronir lived a boy born for great things.

More chuckling, followed by a hushing noise.

Magnai was his name. A full measure bigger and quieter than most youths his age, possessed of a fearsome strength that rivaled that of a full-grown warrior. He could carry a half-dozen pails of milk with ease, and wield an axe twice his size as if it were a hatchet. So talented was he that he often joined the men in their hunts, leading them to laugh and proclaim that Magnai was destined to be named the most radiant. Such things would be decided in the brotherly contests, of course, but still they patted his head and showered him with praise, which he enjoyed, as any boy would.

But what the young warrior loved to hear most of all were the tales of antiquity.

Again and again he would pester the storytellers to recount the oldest of them all—that of the Father and the Mother, their war and their children. With wide eyes and open ears he would sit as the elders spoke of the love that had blossomed between the children of Azim and Nhaama, and how the gods had come to share in it as well. Of how the gods could never be together, and of how the avatar of Azim, he of midnight scale, came to dwell amongst Nhaama's children as protector, giving rise to the Oronir.

Every time the storyteller reached the conclusion of the tale, Magnai would nod powerfully in affirmation, and return to his training without a word, his resolve forged anew.

Until, one day, after the tale had been told, Brother Magnai asked a question.

"Elder, how will I know when I have met my Nhaama?"

One with a skin to his lips nearly chokes on his drink.

Magnai's question, of course, stemmed from the Oroniri belief that the Dusk Mother, upon seeing the children of the Dawn Father, shed tears of love and longing, which upon striking the ground, rose up as counterparts to the men. For every sun, there would be a moon, for every Azim a Nhaama.

Surprised, the storyteller began to tell Magnai of how he met his true love. But Magnai grew restless, for the humble tale was a far cry from the ancient legends he held in such high regard.

So Magnai went and asked his older brothers, "How will I know when I have met my Nhaama?"

"In the markets," one said. "Our eyes had but to meet, and it was plain."

"On the hunt," said another. "When I saw her draw her bow, I knew at once that it was her."

He heard many such tales. A chance meeting, a shared glance. And then all was as it should be.

But like the storyteller before them, their accounts told Magnai nothing. From the smiling faces of those men who had been shown favor by the gods, who had gone forth and met their moons, he gleaned no secret wisdom.

But Magnai was a boy of faith. In his heart he knew that he was bound by fate to a woman of the dusk, and that when they met, they would both know.

Magnai's thoughts often turned to his Nhaama and what sort of person she might be. The Steppe is vast, and the Xaela many. She could be anywhere, among any tribe, he feared.

Now, Magnai had many sisters, and they were no less formidable than he. Whenever he tried to sneak away to play, in neglect of his chores, they would not rest until they had tracked him down. Once discovered, he would whine and protest, for he cared not for such menial tasks, but they saw to it that he completed each and every one—for which he liked them not at all.

One day, as he sullenly tended to wool freshly dyed by his elder sisters, he mused that his moon would never raise her voice to him as they did. Nay, she would be a gentle, ethereal maiden.

Murmurs, a snide remark.

Aye, that would be the perfect wife.

Later, Magnai was sent out alone by his sisters to bring home a lost lamb. As the burning sun sank low on the horizon, the boy came upon a horde of halgai thick as summer grass, drawn by the bleating of his quarry. He waded through the beasts and saved the lamb, of course, but by then the stars were out, and Magnai had no choice but to take shelter amidst the rocks with the animal and wait out the freezing night.

He woke as the Dawn Father's growing light began to blot out that of the stars. He watched as the world was transformed by the grace of Azim, as the sky grew brighter and brighter, like the cheeks of a blushing maiden, and the sight filled his heart with joy.

He mused that his moon would be this beautiful, and to look on her would be to relive this moment. She would be a dancer in the morning mist.

A groan followed by a burst of laughter.

Aye, that would be the perfect wife!

Years passed, and the young warrior grew bigger and stronger, and when he was old enough to join in the brotherly contests, he won with ease and was named the eldest. Brimming with power and pride, he led the Oronir to victory in the Naadam, and upon him were heaped still greater accolades. None were more fit to wear midnight scale than he, the most radiant of Azim's sons, the sworn protectors of the Xaela.

But for all his triumphs, for all his glory, he had yet to find his Nhaama.

One sighs; another stands to wander off into the dark and make water.

There were maidens who made overtures, of course. But Magnai was particular—very particular. "Not her," he would say, "Not her," and before long none would even bother to approach him.

One after another, brothers of the same age found their moons, while Magnai sat his throne and brooded, his mood growing fouler with each passing day. Seeing this, one of the younger offered a suggestion.

"Most radiant brother Magnai, 'twas you who led the Oronir to victory in the Naadam, you who claimed the Dawn Throne, you who rose above all others on the Steppe! Surely it is within your power to demand that the maidens of these lands come before you, is it not? Let us send horse and yol to the far corners of the Steppe, and by the grace of Father Azim, they will return with your Nhaama!"

It was, Magnai saw, a wise suggestion.

Many maidens of the Steppe answered Magnai's call. In the shadow of the Dawn Throne, they gathered to present themselves to the most radiant, who sat in a grand pavilion with an expression most severe. At his shoulder stood one of the younger, who leaned forward and whispered in his ear.

"Most radiant brother Magnai, I give you the fairest maidens of the Steppe. I have no doubt that one among them is descended from the tears of the Dusk Mother and destined to stand at your side."

At this, Magnai nodded, before rising from his seat to inspect the line of women. He looked from left to right, studying their faces. Some looked on him with awe. Others with unease. Others still with disgust. But his eye was quickly drawn to one above all the rest.

Despite the mask she wore to cover her mouth, her beauty was plain to see. She did not share whispers with those next to her, nor did she watch him with fear like some. She was calm and composed and stood in silence, seemingly oblivious to his presence.

Magnai was intrigued. "You there," he began, stepping forward. The woman, however, stepped back with a start.

Alas, the most radiant had had few dealings with the Qestir, and was unaware that the woman had no interest in him—only his pavilion, which would surely have attracted many customers in Reunion.

A chorus of laughter, followed by calls for quiet.

Annoyed and confused, Magnai seized the woman's wrist. She froze, her eyes wide in terror.

She was weak and he was strong, and he could easily have crushed her arm had that been his intention. He himself was surprised to discover this. Still he held fast to the maiden's wrist. She was not unlike his sisters in stature, but she was graceful, and had yet to raise her voice to him. He felt his heart beat faster. *Could she be the one?* he wondered.

Magnai stared at her, as if searching for the answer. Searching for the color in her cheeks, waiting for her to lift her head and look into his eyes and reveal the moon of whom he had dreamt for so long. He would offer a thousand prayers in the gods' names then and there, and that day he would make plans for the greatest wedding ceremony the Steppe had ever seen…

Oh, if only!

For the trembling maiden, shrinking beneath Magnai's steely gaze, burst into tears and shook her head fervently in refusal! And in that instant, a voice thick with venom, a voice like thunder echoed around the Steppe!

"Ha ha ha ha! There, you have your answer! Now, let her go. Unless you joy in making girls cry?"

All turned to the woman standing apart from the others. A woman clad in the blue of the undying ones come not to offer herself, but to observe the farce. Fearless, she strode forward, white hair dancing in the breeze.

She was Sadu, khatun of the Dotharl, who had fought many times against the Oronir for supremacy of the Steppe.

Smiles and nods of approval and respect.

Eyes wide, nostrils flaring, Magnai released the Qestiri maiden, who bowed her head in thanks to Sadu and rejoined the other women, who were observing the coming confrontation at a distance.

"So this is the Oronir's new khan. Though we did not meet on the field of battle, I heard tales of your feats…but none of your other appetites. How disappointing."

"Mannerless gedan. Do not presume to understand things of which you know nothing. Leave…or join the others, if you will. The sun may yet show you favor."

Sadu bared her teeth in a grin—a blue-eyed baras toying with her prey. She spied several Oroniri brothers approaching, and in a flash drew forth her staff and set the earth ablaze!

The younger shrank back in fear, and the other women fled. But, to his credit, Magnai merely frowned.

"Hah! It seems I have frightened away all your little moons. Or maybe they were grateful for the excuse?" She spread her arms wide and raised her chin, as if basking in the heat of her flames. "Your victory changes nothing. The world will not bend to your whims—much less we Dotharl!"

She lowered her head, and her eyes were full of murder and joy.

A brother raced to his side and pressed his great axe into his hand before withdrawing once more, for this was between the khan and the khatun.

"One day," he was heard to whisper then. "One day I shall find you, my love. My lady of the dusk. My ethereal maiden. My dancer in the morning mist."

Three days and three nights their battle raged—for as long as the Oronir had fought to claim the Dawn Throne. In the end, however, neither one could best the other, and Sadu Khatun returned home to lick her wounds and dream of vengeance.

And the most radiant brother? He too returned to his home—to the brothers whose happiness he still envied, and the throne he would sit alone. All, all alone.

But who can say what the future holds?

Tales from the Storm

The Players and the Pawns

Tataru tells herself it will all end well, and in her heart of hearts, she knows it probably will.

As she strolls through the bustling streets of Kugane, winding her way towards the Ruby Bazaar, she thinks back to the young man she had bid farewell to on the pier. Before boarding the ship, Alphinaud had said a great many things, most of which amounted to "For the Twelve's sakes, be careful." And she will, of course, for Tataru Taru is no fool—far from it—and woe betide the scheming merchant who dares to try and outwit *her*. Woe betide them very much indeed.

She mounts the steps and pushes past the doors into the Ruby Bazaar, glancing at the aide behind the counter, who bows in recognition and bids her proceed into an adjoining room. There she finds a bespectacled blond gentleman waiting to receive her, steaming cup of tea in hand.

"Ah…" he sighs theatrically, "Master Alphinaud will be sorely missed."

Tataru smiles and agrees, being an agreeable sort—or rather being quite good at affecting the appearance.

"Shall we move on to the matter of the aetheryte components, then?"

This surprises her, as she does not recall ever having discussed the subject before.

"Did we not? I could have sworn that we did."

Of course, how forgetful of her. Surely they did, for how else could he possibly know? And so they speak of what is required to restore the broken aetheryte in the House of the Fierce; how such materials might be procured and delivered to their allies in Yanxia, and—most importantly—the question of cost.

Hancock flashes a smile and inclines his head ever so slightly. "I pray you will forgive my boldness, but I have taken the liberty of arranging a meeting between you and two representatives of trading concerns which can supply you with the components you seek."

Again, this surprises her. Perhaps he sees it in her face as he continues.

"I am given to understand you are a fearsome negotiator, and I thought you might relish the opportunity to do what you do best."

Tataru cannot help but grin, as she would relish it a great deal.

The table in the upper level of the hostelry affords privacy, after a fashion.

The cacophony below, while muted, provides a measure of protection from eavesdropping. Not that Tataru is particularly concerned about such things, for aetherytes are scattered throughout the Far East, and various parties have a vested interest in their continued upkeep. Not just the Scions and the Liberation Front, oh no.

Across from her sit two men. Two choices—hers ostensibly, but theirs ultimately. The Hannish trader cuts a flamboyant figure, draped in silks and with a dyed shock of hair. His counterpart, an older Hingan man, favors more traditional, austere garments of the Far Eastern fashion. But he is not without his indulgences, judging from the imported clockwork timepiece with which he fiddles while shifting in his seat.

Tataru begins the meeting with the requisite pleasantries and polite inquiries before beginning negotiations in earnest. She explains in detail what components are desired. Shipment will not be required, despite the Hannish trader's generous offer to provide a discount should she allow his men to deliver them to their destination. This pains her, but Hancock was most insistent that the company handle transport, and on this point Alphinaud agreed. Used and refurbished will not suffice, for Alphinaud and Alisaie will take no chances with faulty parts. The Hingan warns her that this will increase the cost significantly, though his pained expression when the Han says otherwise is telling.

But this is all little more than a prelude to the main event. Satisfied she knows everything she needs to know, she thanks the pair for their time and bids them good day.

The Han is first to speak. "Mistress Tataru, where are you going? You have not yet heard my proposal!" She waves him off, stating that neither he nor his Hingan counterpart could possibly offer terms as attractive as those already set out by her preferred provider.

While the flamboyant merchant gropes about for words, it is the solemn Hingan who abruptly blurts out a figure. At this, the Han whirls round, his face a picture of betrayed indignation. She can see the gears turning in his head as he works his jaw silently, before shooting her a sidelong glance. Tataru raises an expectant eyebrow.

"Well! Let it not be said I am unreasonable," he begins, and ends with a figure marginally less than the Hingan's.

153

It goes on like this for a time, Tataru interjecting where appropriate to keep the two at each other's throats. The cards matter less than the hands that hold them, and every nervous twitch, every unconscious gesture speaks volumes to her. But while the Han is a prisoner to pride, the Hingan is driven by desperation. He *needs* this contract, costs be damned, and so it is he who wins the day by halving his initial offer.

The Hannish trader can only throw up his hands in exasperated defeat. "To go any lower would be to cut my own throat—and I am in business to secure a *living* for myself, not an early death." And so he departs in a huff, leaving Tataru and his rival to finalize the details.

After watching him go, the Hingan turns to her wearing a look of ill-concealed relief. "May this be but the first of many profitable arrangements," he says.

It will not be.

Although Hancock is effusive in his praise, Tataru takes little joy in it. She has every reason to be proud, given the unconscionably low price she had agreed to pay, and yet there is a lingering sense that she has not exceeded his expectations, but fulfilled them. Nevertheless, she finds herself humming as she saunters to the pier to collect the components some few days later. With any luck, she will have them on a ship bound for Yanxia before sunset.

The storehouse is unattended when she arrives. The door is slightly ajar, however, and while she sees only darkness within, she pokes her head inside, calling out to whoever may be present. Receiving no answer, she shrugs and crosses the threshold.

Tataru squints as her eyes slowly adjust to the low light, but this incremental progress is lost when the door is abruptly slammed shut behind her. The sudden impact sends her tumbling to the ground, and as she struggles to regain her feet, she hears metal on metal without. She rushes to the door, finds it locked, and begins pounding on the heavy wood with her fists while crying for help, though she fears that the only ones who can hear her are the ones holding the key.

Alone in the dark, her imagination runs wild. A dozen scenarios present themselves, each more elaborate than the last: conspiracies grand

and far-reaching, and she reduced to a pawn in the great game. But whose great game? Hancock's? It was he who arranged for her to meet with the merchants, was it not? Did he know, then? Was this his design?

She sits in the dirt and leans against the storehouse door, straining to make sense of the muffled sounds beyond the thick wooden planks. Whispers, she thinks, low and nervous. An indeterminate moment later, another voice, familiar, calling out from a distance. Jovial. Co-conspirators? Footsteps, unhurried. Then others, all of a sudden, from other directions. Conversation, louder now, tinged with emotion. With anger. Shouting now, first with words, then without. A shuffling of feet, a sharp crack accompanied by a gasp. A dull, wet thud. And then, silence.

Softly, Tataru hears footsteps approaching the door. She has held her breath hostage since first she heard sounds of struggle, and it aches to escape. Not yet, not yet. Closer now, the footsteps come, stopping just outside the door. The pounding of her heart fills her head, but still she can hear the jingle of keys, and then she is falling backwards as the door upon which she had been leaning is yanked open.

Dazzled, she find herself flat on her back, just outside the storeroom entrance, her head at the feet of someone she dearly hopes is her savior. Silhouetted against the noonday sun, the figure standing over her bends down and proffers a hand. Squinting, she at last makes out the upside-down face of a man. A blond man.

"My sincerest apologies for keeping you waiting, my dear."

She closes her eyes, takes a deep breath, and bites her tongue.

In fairness, Hancock apologizes again later and at length for not taking Tataru into his confidence. At the Ruby Bazaar, after the dust has settled, he sits her down and explains how the Hingan merchant had become indebted to Frumentarium agents, who had subsequently directed him to establish a relationship with the Scions. When Hancock put the word out that he sought to obtain aetheryte components for a client, the merchant rightly assumed that it was on Tataru's behalf, and so he called at the Ruby Bazaar.

"Lest you wonder, I didn't know he was their cat's-paw. Not for a certainty, at least."

This does not placate her. As she nurses her tea, Tataru frowns and accuses him of using her as bait.

"Please. It never crossed my mind that he would be so stupid as to attempt to kidnap you on the Garleans' behalf. Frankly, I doubt very much it crossed theirs either."

She wonders aloud why he had his Brass Blades shadow her, then.

"Hope for the best, prepare for the worst," he says simply, and she can only shrug in agreement.

Embarrassed though she is, she has little reason to remain angry with Hancock. The treacherous Hingan merchant and his cronies are in the care of the Sekiseigumi, and no longer pose a threat. Moreover, despite his nefarious intentions, the Hingan had gone so far as to procure the aetheryte parts she requested, perhaps in an effort to maintain the ruse. In the chaos following her detainment and liberation, said components found their way into her possession, courtesy of the Brass Blades—and at no charge, at that. Indeed, it is remarkable how everything seems to have worked out for the best.

And yet, one question yet weighs on her mind...

"The storehouse? Why, I believe the *bugyosho* will auction off the contents and rent it to a new client. And since we were instrumental in bringing disruptive foreign agents to justice, I expect the East Aldenard Trading Company will be afforded right of first refusal. Not that we would—space is ever at a premium in Kugane..."

Tataru sighs. It will all end well, she tells herself. Whether she likes it or not.

When the Wager Pays Off

Carried aloft by icy winds, the piping voice of a distant soldier drifted across the Lochs.

"Oh, this crate'll make a coffer when the wager pays off,
Or this crate'll make a coffin when the wager falls through... ♪ "

Pipin knew the song well, as did every Ul'dahn over a certain age. It told the tale of a youth on the way to seek his fortune in the golden city, with only a box for company. His perilous journey through the wilds was depicted as a spirited roll of the dice, an invitation to Nald'thal to fill his burdensome crate with gold, or failing that, his mortal remains.

The marshal had always doubted that the hero of the tale had won his wager, largely because the song had been a favorite of his father's, and he could not think of the man without bracing himself for some impending disaster.

In stark contrast to his adoptive parent, Pipin's birth father was an abject failure—an inveterate gambler and a drunk who would sooner sell his own son than repay a debt with his own sweat. A man who had, in fact, done just that. Pipin had been twelve years old at the time, busily sorting rocks at the mine when he was accosted by a brawny lanista.

"Come, boy—you belong to me now! And the bloodsands ever thirst!"

And before he knew what was happening, the young Lalafell found himself sprawled on the floor of a cramped stone cell in the gladiator stables. Days of ceaseless drudgery were to follow. Every morning, he was awoken at the crack of dawn to perform chores for the older fighters. And when those duties were done, he could look forward to hours in the practice yard under the gaze of the merciless drillmaster, the slightest mistake corrected by the snap of a whip or the thud of a cudgel.

The only thing Pipin *didn't* hate about his new life was the food. A gladiator's body was an investment, and the lanista wanted his charges fit and strong to bring home his share of the prize money. Even the novices were provided with hearty meals: great slabs of bread, and fist-sized chunks of meat swimming in broth. Better still, the cook was liberal in his use of spices, treating Pipin's palate to a world of flavors he never knew existed.

But beyond that single pleasure, the pain of each passing day seemed ever more difficult to bear. Pipin wasn't sure how long he could endure the grueling routine, and even if he did, there was no guarantee that he would survive his first match on the sands.

I am no better than a slave.

Desperate to escape, Pipin watched and waited for a chance to run away, but the drillmaster never once seemed to relax his guard. It seemed there was no way out but the grave. Then, after a year of backbreaking labor and bone-crunching training, he was ordered to serve as an attendant to one of the stable's champions. It was a meeting that would change Pipin's life forever, though it hardly seemed momentous at the time…

"How old are you, lad?"

"Thirteen."

The gladiator seemed satisfied with Pipin's answer, and made no further effort to engage him in conversation during their walk to one of the Coliseum's antechambers. Unsure if the rugged Highlander was nervous before his match or merely a man of few words, the boy resolved to hold his tongue. Gladiators could be a foul-tempered lot, and Pipin did not wish to earn himself a clip around the ear for breaking this one's focus.

Even after arriving in the antechamber the Highlander said nothing save for a few terse instructions. Pipin carried them out wordlessly, helping to strap the gladiator into his armor, before finally proffering his helm; a piece styled to resemble a bull's horned head. The towering Hyur plucked it from his hands as if it weighed nothing, pulled it on, and strode out into the arena.

"My lords, ladies, and gentlemen—I give you Raubahn Aldynn, the Bull of Ala Mhigo!"

The ringing voice of the Coliseum herald was answered by a thunderous roar that shook the walls of the antechamber. Pipin was dumbfounded. This "Bull of Ala Mhigo" had merely to set foot on the sands to send the spectators into a frenzy.

In the months that followed, Pipin often found himself acting as Raubahn's attendant. Though the gladiator was reticent at first, their stilted exchanges gradually grew longer, and the pair came to share the

161

details of their past. The Highlander spoke of his birth in the land of Ala Mhigo, and of the battles he had fought—of his people's rebellion against a tyrannous king, and of the Garlean Empire's subsequent invasion. He told of how he had fled his homeland, desperate and wounded. Of how he had stumbled through the wilds until he reached the city of Ul'dah, where he was imprisoned on suspicion of espionage. And now here he was: a Coliseum champion, fighting for his freedom before a crowd who chanted his name.

It seemed inexplicable to Pipin that a man of Raubahn's strength and charisma had been forced into the brutal life of a gladiator. But the thought did not bring him despair. On the contrary, he was encouraged by the idea that a slave of the bloodsands might win enough purses to purchase his own emancipation—that he could be the master of his own fate.

If my fellow slave can buy his freedom, then why not me?

His purpose clear at last, Pipin attended to his training with new determination. He would survive. He would be free.

"Here it is! I have the final payment in my hand!"

The look of triumph on Raubahn's face as he strode back into the antechamber would linger long in Pipin's memory. The Highlander seemed happier than after all of his previous victories combined. *And little wonder...*

"Never was a prize more well-deserved!" Pipin exclaimed, beaming.

He need never set foot on the bloodsands again. The mere thought of it made him giddy. But in that same moment came the realization—the certainty that the man who had so transformed his outlook, the mentor in whose footsteps he longed to tread, would soon be gone.

"Why are you frowning, lad?" Raubahn asked, confused. "You're free."

Now it was Pipin's turn to look confused. They stood frozen for a moment in an awkward tableau: a hulking gladiator clutching a bulging prize purse staring down in consternation at an equally puzzled Lalafell youth.

"I'm saying you needn't risk your life anymore," Raubahn went on, a hint of exasperation in his voice. "Most young gladiators never get to be old. Pit two against each other, and both are apt to end up dead. I would spare you that fate."

Realization finally dawned. Over the months since their first meeting, the Highlander had not been setting his winnings against the price of his own freedom. *He has been paying off Father's debt.* Pipin's eyes filled with tears as fear and exhaustion—his constant companions for a year and more—were swept away by waves of relief and gratitude. He would toil for the lanista no longer.

The following morning, Pipin stood alone at the gates to the gladiator stables, his meager possessions gathered in a small burlap sack. Raubahn could not leave his cell, and it seemed that neither the lanista nor the drillmaster cared much for a youth in whose future they had no further investment.

Pipin walked out onto the street. The desert sun had scarcely broken the horizon, and the cobblestones felt cool beneath his feet. *Free.* He took three deliberate steps, savoring his unexpected liberation, and then settled into a stroll. But with every footfall along the empty thoroughfare, he became more aware of the niggling doubt in his belly. *What if Father wagers all on another losing cause?* His wine-sodden sire had already shown a willingness to sell off his only child—there was nothing to prevent him from doing so again. *Never.* Pipin came to an abrupt stop, turned on his heels, and set off back the way he had come.

"Pipin, lad? I thought you'd be long gone by now."

Raubahn tilted his head as the small figure at the door to his cell took a deep breath.

"I wish to continue my training as a gladiator," Pipin declared, his voice clear and unwavering. "I am grateful for all you have done for me, but I will never truly be free until I have the strength to free myself."

Pipin duly explained how his father might very well sell him as chattel once more, and that he would rather be the master of his own destiny, however brutal, and learn at the feet of a man he truly respected, than live in fear. Raubahn gave his answer with a fierce grin.

Though well-acquainted with the man's generosity, Pipin was nevertheless astonished by what the gladiator did next. Pipin's father, it transpired, had signed a contract when handing over his son to the lanista, transferring all his rights and obligations as the boy's legal guardian. Drawing on his prize money, Raubahn bought this document from Pipin's former owner, and invoked the guardian clause, thus beginning formal adoption proceedings.

In the years that followed, the pair lived together, as imprisoned father and emancipated son. A curious arrangement, to be sure, but one which allowed Pipin to resume his study of the blade under Raubahn's decidedly less callous tutelage. But despite Pipin's protestations, his adoptive father would not permit him to fight on the sands. Raubahn swore, however, that his path would be his own to choose once he came of age.

Now twenty-five years old, seasoned by a stint as a mercenary, Pipin was an officer of the Immortal Flames, fighting to reclaim Raubahn's beloved homeland.

"You risked much and more to see me thrive, Father," Pipin said, unsheathing Tizona's heavy blade. "And I will see that your wager pays off!"

The Weight of a Name

"Just like that, then. Another squadron. Lost."

Conrad's shoulders sagged as he sighed and muttered under his breath. *Cursing the gods or himself?* M'naago watched his eyes. They looked past her, past everything. *What do you see? The faces of the poor bastards you ordered to East End, I'll bet. Some of our best.*

None had survived the ambush.

The Ala Mhigan Resistance comprised countless factions, and the people of Rhalgr's Reach were but one. By its nature, it could never truly be defeated by the imperial army. Nevertheless, the loss of so many experienced soldiers, some of whom had fought for nearly twenty years, would be keenly felt. *Even a bloody novice like me can see that.* M'naago cleared her throat.

"We don't know if the imperials found the tunnel, sir, but even if they didn't…without our men to guide them, our friends from Ul'dah are likely stranded."

Out of the corner of her eye, M'naago spied Meffrid, frowning. *Well, if you're not going to say it…*

"Sir, if I may…who *are* these people, and why are we risking so much to get them on the wrong side of Baelsar's bloody Wall?"

The obvious question was answered with folded arms and furtive glances. After a time, Conrad spoke.

"They're Scions of the Seventh Dawn. Old friends. One is the daughter of Curtis Hext."

The voice of the rebellion? The man who spat in the mad king's eye? M'naago wasn't sure what answer she had expected, but this wasn't it. *Bloody novice indeed…*

"Name's Yda," Conrad continued. "After the occupation, she fled to Sharlayan. Learned a lot there, I'm told, but she never forgot about us. Yda's been assisting us for years now, as a Scion."

M'naago had heard about the Scions. The "Saviors of Eorzea," some had called them. But they had become embroiled in the political machinations of Ul'dah's elite, and now people were saying that they had assassinated the sultana. It seemed that Yda and her companion had reached out to the Resistance seeking a means to escape justice. *The East End squadron was their last hope…*

Or so M'naago thought.

"Nothing for it but to go and get them ourselves," Conrad said.

The leaves twisted and twirled as they tumbled to the ground, traced by two pairs of eyes in the brush.

"All this for two people. It's not like him."

M'naago knelt, an arrow notched in her bow, trying desperately to ignore her own heartbeat. *Gods, I hate the waiting.*

"Trust in the old bear. He wouldn't take the risk if it wasn't worth it."

Meffrid, who had been tasked with training M'naago, was ever the voice of reason. He had told her before of how the Scions were instrumental in the Eorzean Alliance's campaign against the XIVth Legion—of how their forces had led an assault on Castrum Meridianum during Operation Archon, in which Gaius van Baelsar was killed. Such powerful allies would be invaluable in enlisting the support of the Alliance, without whom they could not hope to liberate Ala Mhigo. M'naago scowled.

"If you say so…"

Meffrid glanced at her sidelong, then sighed.

"Just between us, I reckon he's got a mind to recruit her. Maybe even groom her for a leading role."

"Who? Yda?"

"Think about it. The daughter of a revolutionary hero, returned to fight for her homeland's freedom? Now that's a tale that'll move men's hearts. That's a banner people'll flock to."

A bard's tale, aye. Some girl who's been away for twenty years. Just what we need.

"Symbols have power," he continued. "Heard of the Griffin?"

She nodded. *Mad bastard and his Masks are preaching bloody vengeance to all and sundry.* None knew his true identity, though some claimed he was a distant relative of Theodoric. Some even thought that was a good thing. *Anyone's better than the Garleans, eh? Sod that. We've had enough of kings.*

A hawk's cry rang out.

"Time to go, lass. Up, up!"

The pair broke cover and ran towards the rocks. The entrance was well concealed and showed no signs of recent use. A short while later, as they crawled on their hands and knees through a narrow tunnel dug more than a decade before, M'naago recalled stories of imperial sabotage and bodies buried beneath a mountain of earth and stone. She thought of Conrad and the others. *Fighting right now. Dying right now, maybe.*

You'd better be worth it.

The pair were in a bad way when they finally limped into the Reach. And what a pair they were. Bleeding and bickering, still fuming over some great betrayal back in Ul'dah, worried sick about their comrades, from whom they had been separated in the chaos. But a week at the Barber's did wonders for their disposition. To a point.

Papalymo, the thaumaturge, invariably assumed he was the cleverest person in the room—an attitude made all the more annoying by the fact that he invariably was. Yda, on the other hand, was reckless and impulsive. Emotional. But she had a way with people—a way of making them smile and think everything was going to be all right…

Both the Scions were eager to lend a hand and repay the Resistance, and it was not long before M'naago came to view them as friends and comrades in arms. But when she thought back to what Meffrid had said about Conrad's designs—about grooming Yda as a leader, she just couldn't see it. Not yet…

It was a day like any other. M'naago and Yda had been tasked with reconnoitering Castrum Oriens, and they were preparing to return home when a high-pitched wail cut through the silence.

"A woman?" hissed the scout, suddenly alert. "No…a girl!"

The villages in East End had long been abandoned, and only imperial soldiers traveled the roads. *No one in their right mind ought to be out here…*

"Let's go, M'naago!"

Yda was already running. *Godsdammit.* M'naago tried to keep up, then settled for trying to keep her companion in sight.

After running what felt like malms, they arrived at the foot of a great tree. Lying at its roots was an older man, unconscious, bleeding from countless wounds. He was wearing Resistance colors. Before him, a little girl stood sobbing. *Followed the trail of blood, did you…?*

Realization dawned.

"Seven hells, I think he's one of the squadron we dispatched to meet you a month back! I thought there were no survivors."

Yda knelt beside the man and began tending to his wounds. "There'll be time for questions later," she said, without turning. "Take the girl and head back to the Reach."

M'naago blinked. "Eh?"

"Papalymo told me about this tactic. He's bait. The imperials probably heard the girl too. They'll be here any moment."

"Then we've got to get out of here! Both of us! That or we both stay and fight!"

"The girl's not part of this. Someone has to take her. And this man's one of ours. We can't just leave him here!"

M'naago glared at Yda. *Three fighters—one at death's door—and a crying little girl. All in the shadow of a bloody castrum.*

Godsdammit.

M'naago grabbed the girl by the arm and tried to drag her away. She simply stood there, frozen. *Godsdammit it all.* M'naago scooped the child up and flung her over her shoulder.

"Stay alive. I'll be back."

And then she ran.

M'naago wound her way north through the forest, her mind racing. *Get the girl to safety, call for reinforcements— Movement!*

She ducked behind a tree and strained to listen.

"She can't have gone far!" shouted a voice.

Woman, distraught. Ala Mhigan. Mother. Thank the Twelve.

The woman wore hunter's leathers and had a bow slung across her back. She stared when she first saw M'naago, but ran towards her when she recognized the girl cradled in her arms. She tried to thank her as she took the girl from M'naago, but the scout had already turned and started running back the way she had come.

You'd better still be alive…

171

Bodies lay strewn about the clearing. Men and women clad in steel and black cloth. *A whole patrol...*

They were all dead.

Carefully, she stepped over and between them, eyes fixed on the sole figure that still stood, streaked with mud and blood and panting like a feral beast.

It whirled at her approach, fists raised, teeth bared, growling low.

By Rhalgr...

Time seemed to stand still for a moment...then Yda let her arms fall to her sides and sank to her knees, her face a picture of dismay.

"Papalymo's never going to let me hear the end of this."

And indeed, the thaumaturge would chastise Yda when they returned to Rhalgr's Reach. Nor could she blame him. It was stupid and reckless and impossible to justify, and yet... And yet...

Days later, after Yda had time to recover, M'naago found her one night standing at Starfall's shore and staring up at the Destroyer. She asked the Scion, then and there, if she would consider joining the Resistance. But Yda refused.

"Funnily enough, you're not even the first person to ask. I said no to Conrad too."

"But why? This is your homeland—this is your fight! I mean, for godssakes—you're the daughter of Curtis Hext! People'll follow you, don't you see?"

Yda bowed her head, then looked again to the towering statue of Rhalgr.

"I'm his daughter—not him. I may not know a lot of things, but I know that's not enough."

M'naago opened her mouth to protest, but couldn't find the words.

"Papalymo and I have still got friends out there. Good people we've fought beside time and again. After we find them, we'll work together to make it right."

She turned to her and smiled.

"That's all that matters in the end, isn't it, Naago?"

At first, she wasn't sure how to respond. But M'naago found herself smiling back. *What does it matter what we call each other*, she thought— both then and later, when Lyse told her the truth about her sister and the mask and everything else.

You're still the same woman. The same friend. I'll fight with you.
And I'll follow you too.

From Azure Ashes

The breeze that caressed the ruined palace seemed tinged with gold.

More than anything else, it was said that the great wyrm Ratatoskr loved to weave songs, and the eldritch power of her verses still lingered here, a thousand years after her voice was forever silenced by the treachery of mortals. In the wake of her death, the dragons had named her home in the clouds Sohr Khai, words that mean "grieving apology," out of guilt over their failure to protect her, and left the place untouched.

A lone figure took in the scene before kneeling to lay a bouquet.

"I know I make for a strange messenger…but the war is over."

It was, he conceded, an awkward utterance. But how could it be otherwise? What else could he say to the she-wyrm whose murder had kindled the flames of the Dragonsong War—he whose sole purpose in life had been to hunt her kind? *Sorry…?* Even as he struggled to fashion an apology, a sudden gust scattered his offering of flowers, sending petals billowing in all directions.

"I did not expect to find thee here, Azure Dragoon."

Estinien did not so much hear the voice as feel it echoing inside his mind. But he both heard and felt the beating of mighty wings that followed. Looking up, he beheld a familiar white form descending. *Hraesvelgr… So much for privacy.*

Following Nidhogg's defeat and his miraculous rescue upon the Steps of Faith, Estinien had remained in the Holy See only long enough to witness his old friend Aymeric appointed lord speaker of the House of Lords. He had then quietly taken his leave, not with a mind to forsake his homeland, but to ponder how he might serve it in this new age. With the war at an end, he reasoned, his presence was no longer required. There was no place for a man who had spilled as much dragon blood as he, much less one who had turned lance and fang upon his own people as his enemy's thrall.

Whereto, then, for Ishgard's unwanted champion? Estinien could think of several places. And so he had embarked upon a journey.

To the ruins of Ferndale, the village of his birth, to offer a prayer to his beloved mother, father, and little brother, Hamignant. To a cliff overlooking the capital, to give thanks to the knight brave and true whose sacrifice had kept Ishgard's hopes alive. To the floating continent,

Azys Lla, to pay tribute to the maiden of conviction who blazed a path for her comrades by burning the candle of her life.

His old self would never have contemplated such a sentimental journey. But times had changed, and so had he. Last of all, he had come to Sohr Khai, to voice his regret to the long-departed Ratatoskr. A visit he had hoped would go unnoticed.

"Spying ill becomes you, wyrm," Estinien growled.

The great wyrm's muzzle contorted into what must have been a smile.

"Ah, do I intrude? I but desired to show mine appreciation for thy gesture. My brood-sister would have welcomed it."

For a time, Estinien's soul had been merged with that of Nidhogg; the dread wyrm's tumultuous storm of emotions comingling with his own. The rancor, the fury, the grief—he had felt it all. And the grief lingered even now. The gulf left behind by Ratatoskr's passing was one he knew as well as any man or dragon. And thus were Hraesvelgr's words more comforting than the wyrm realized.

"I am owed no such kindness. But…thank you," Estinien replied, his voice catching in his throat. Gathering himself, he continued, "And for what it is worth, I am Azure Dragoon no longer. This age has no need of my lance."

At this, the great wyrm's eyes narrowed.

"And yet there it is upon thy back, fair dripping with my brood-brother's essence."

The observation caught him wholly unawares. When he had left Ishgard behind, he had done so without his dragoon's armor, deeming it a relic of a former life. Yet somehow it had not occurred to him to likewise lay down his lance, warped though it was by Nidhogg's power. Estinien's confoundment was plain to Hraesvelgr, and when he spoke, it was in tones tinged with the faintest trace of pity.

"Thy fight is not over, mortal. As thou knowest only too well."

The sting of another realization.

Damn you, wyrm. He had the right of it, of course. Azure Dragoon or no, there was still work to be done. Purpose even for a lance tempered and honed in an unjust war.

"If thou wouldst swear to fight for man and dragon both, then come with me. Unto thee I shall bequeath armor befitting a *true* dragoon."

Without waiting for a response, Hraesvelgr leapt into the sky with a powerful kick, his tattered wings bearing him away so swiftly that his looming form soon became no more than a speck in the heavens. Snapping out of his reverie, Estinien dashed to his manacutter and took off in pursuit.

After a brief flight, they came to a cluster of ruins upon the fringes of Sohr Khai; a stable for wyverns during the forgotten days of harmony, Estinien guessed. There the great wyrm landed, and after he had followed suit, Hraesvelgr nodded towards the heart of the ruins. They had not walked far when Estinien caught sight of what he knew at once to be their destination.

"By the Fury…"

Inside what appeared to be the remains of a barracks built for men sat several armory chests. All bore the scars of the inexorable march of time save one—a pristine example, preserved by some manner of draconic enchantment. Estinien needed no further encouragement.

As he approached the chest, Hraesvelgr broke the silence. "In the beginning, dragoons were men who fought beside dragons, not against them. Ratatoskr took great pleasure in bearing such fearless souls upon her back. And thus did she bless their armor with her power."

Lifting the lid, Estinien's jaw fell open. Before him lay not one but two magnificent suits of plate armor. Their hue was all too familiar. *Azure. Gods forgive me…*

"At first, men felt honored to receive such gifts. But the more power they received, the more they craved. And all too soon, naught save the source of that power would sate them."

And so they butchered her… Devoured her eyes like feral beasts.

The armor of the first dragoons, brimming with power freely given… The mere sight of it made Estinien's heart swell. But he made no move to claim his prize.

"Why?" he said at length. "Why grant *me* this power? What makes you think I am any different from Thordan and the rest?"

At this, the wyrm paused, head lowered, before answering softly, "A maiden did give me cause to believe in thy kind once more." Only after another lengthy silence did he continue. "Never was this armor worn. It wanteth for a master—a true dragoon. Thou hast cast aside one azure. If thou wouldst take up another, it is thine."

A short while later, Estinien emerged from the barracks with new armor and newfound purpose. The azure plate gleamed brilliantly as it caught the light of the midday sun.

"Such armor deserves a name," he declared. "And I know one which befits it well."

Hraesvelgr stared at him expectantly.

"Iceheart. For it shall watch over a man ignorant of all things save how to wield a lance steeped in anger."

At these words, Hraesvelgr threw back his head and let loose a mighty roar, both of approval and amusement. The dragoon had chosen well.

When Estinien finally left the Churning Mists, his feet carried him almost of their own volition towards the battlefield once more, there to cut a path for his comrades, whose struggles yet continued.

Time went by, and the war for Ala Mhigo's liberation found the forces of the Eorzean Alliance at the fortress city's doorstep. From his cliffside vantage point, Estinien watched as the host wended its way through the Lochs, a great serpent with soldiers for scales. Though they were too far away to see, he doubted not but that his comrades were among them—Aymeric, Alphinaud, the Warrior of Light. He had silenced the monstrous cannon at Castrum Abania to pave their way; the final act of casting down the Garleans, he left to them.

Something else demanded his attention. A matter for him alone. *Make that two matters*, he inwardly corrected. Spent of aether as they were, it had been no easy task to track them down...

As the final battle was joined and his friends fought on, he quietly intercepted a squadron of flying armor that was moving to flank them. It was then that he felt the call—a power he knew as intimately as he knew himself, emanating from the skies high above the royal palace. Pulling the tip of his lance free of a smoldering wreck, he struck out at a brisk run, making his way through the unfolding chaos. But by the time he finally emerged in the gardens of the Royal Menagerie, it was all over. All save his own task.

Even without seeing them, he knew exactly where they lay. Striding through the exotic flowers, heedless of their beauty, he came to a halt at a patch like any other. And there they were, Nidhogg's eyes, staring blindly up at him.

"Well, well, well, what a fine mess we've made," he greeted them as old friends. "All but spent feeding that primal, eh? Well, you won't be making any mischief with that amount of aether."

He drew his lance—named for his nemesis and the dragon he himself once was—and aimed its deadly point at one helpless eyeball.

"Still…better safe than sorry."

Bracing himself body and soul, he plunged into the eye. It gave way readily, turning into black mist and disappearing into the crimson sky. Wasting no time, he then consigned its twin to the selfsame fate.

"There. There ends your hateful legacy."

Thus did Estinien's journey come to an end—a journey which had seen him revisit the past and in so doing find a future. His lifelong battle having reached its true conclusion, he could finally begin anew. None can say whither his road will lead, whether the skies that greet him will be the striking blue of day, the blazing crimson of dusk, or the deepening black of twilight. Yet wheresoever he should find himself, one thing is certain: he will ever wield his lance for man and dragon both.

Tales from the Storm

A Calm After the Storm

Y'shtola closed her eyes, savoring the flavor and warmth of the tea. It had not been long since the great battle for Ala Mhigo's liberation, but in this moment of blessed respite, it might as well have been an age. The patisserie's unassuming tables and chairs were arranged along one of Limsa Lominsa's coiling decks, offering patrons a fine view of the Rhotano. Eschewing the pomp and ceremony of Limsa's more lauded establishments, it was favored among locals as a place for friends to spend a relaxing afternoon by the sea.

To look at her casually sipping tea, contentment writ upon her face, none would have guessed the trials Y'shtola had recently overcome. As she replaced her cup, a soft chuckle escaped her lips. Spread out before her was an assortment of mouthwatering treats, among them the patisserie's specialty: a rich vanilla tart laden with glistening jam and plump berries. Across the table, Alisaie raised a quizzical eyebrow as she popped another cookie into her mouth. Dusting off her fingers, she scanned the area for the invitees who had yet to arrive. Her eyes settled upon a familiar figure bounding towards them.

"Sorry I'm late!" Lyse exclaimed, breathless.

Y'shtola waved away the apology. "Yours was the longer journey. And we started without you."

With a happy sigh, Lyse flopped into a chair. She was once more dressed in the clothing she had worn during her sojourn in the Far East. This was their first meeting since she had announced her decision to remain in Gyr Abania to aid in rebuilding her homeland, and it was as if a great weight had been lifted from her shoulders. After placing her order with the attending waitress, she turned to regard her friends fondly.

"Gods, it's good to see you!" After a short pause, she continued. "Is this all of us?"

"Krile regrettably cannot attend," Y'shtola explained. "She is in the midst of an important survey and said that she would content herself with a delivery. As for the Warrior of Light…"

Swallowing her cookie, Alisaie picked up where Y'shtola had trailed off, a hint of displeasure in her voice. "Oh, they're doubtless engaged in some heroic endeavor or other. They know the time and place, though, and gave me no reason to believe they wouldn't come."

Lyse's smile was half amusement, half resignation. "The more things change, eh? They never could stay still for long."

Taking this as an invitation, Alisaie gave vent to her frustration. "Isn't that the truth! If they're not cheating death with their fellow adventurers, you can be sure they're off helping the beast tribes, or collecting tomestones, or regaling the children of Idyllshire with the tales of their exploits, or delivering something to someone. Honestly, I don't think they sleep."

Nonplussed by her sudden flash of emotion, Y'shtola and Lyse glanced at one another before bursting out in laughter. Alisaie glared at them, her face a picture of indignation.

"Forgive us," said Y'shtola, with a twinkle in her eye. "We are but impressed by how closely you follow your hero's every act."

"What's that supposed to— I simply asked them what manner of training they undertake! For all the good it did me—none of it is anything I can reasonably emulate."

"Well, I for one wholeheartedly approve of your choice of role model," said Lyse, nodding sagely.

"You too, Lyse? Hmph. If you want to talk about an interesting choice of role model, you should look no further than my brother."

Bringing her fork to bear on her tart, Alisaie proceeded to recount her time in Yanxia…

While Lyse's party traveled to the Azim Steppe in search of Lord Hien, Alisaie and Alphinaud had remained at the House of the Fierce. During that time, her bookish brother had helped to solve the Liberation Front's frequent shortages with a brand of wisdom that could only be described as *useful*.

"When I asked what had prompted him to turn his mind to practical matters, he told me he had met a man who taught him much and more of 'the road,' and that he did not wish to seem idle should their paths chance to cross again. Naturally, he wouldn't say who this mystery man was—only that he saw him as a brother. As if I needed *another* brother to contend with…" Alisaie punctuated the statement by plunging her fork into her tart.

Lyse received the tale of Alphinaud's change with earnest interest, while Y'shtola, having an inkling as to this object of admiration, could only smile wryly. Being a man ungiven to sentiment, she knew, the knowledge that he was missed would do little to hasten his return.

The waitress appeared with Lyse's drink, a glass of lemonade made with honey lemons from Othard. The first sip made her eyes light up, and she followed it with a longer draft. Seeing Lyse's enjoyment took Y'shtola back to her earliest days in Limsa Lominsa, when she was just beginning to discover the city-state's renowned gastronomic culture. For all the culinary knowledge stored in Sharlayan's vast libraries, nothing could replicate the experience of enjoying a delicacy in its native land.

"So, how fare you, Lyse? Has the rebuilding effort begun in earnest?" Y'shtola's question snapped Lyse back to reality, and she lowered both gaze and glass.

"…Sort of. There's no end to the problems, and they're not the kind I can punch. Thinking was always Papalymo's department. I mean, I'm doing my best, but…well, things rarely go to plan." Absently, she ran a finger over the droplets on her glass. "I still catch myself wondering, what would Father do? What would Yda say? Why am I not like them? And I end up making myself depressed." Hearing her own words, Lyse tutted, and fixed Y'shtola with a determined stare. "But I won't give up. Not after everything it took to get this far."

Seeing the fire in Lyse's eyes, Y'shtola could not help but be reminded of Yda when she spoke of liberating her homeland, all those years ago… How proud she would have been.

Letting out a sigh, Alisaie placed a second slice of tart on Lyse's plate.

"But I haven't finished the—"

"You need to keep up your strength," Y'shtola declared, in a tone that brooked no argument. "We all know that working hard makes you hungry. As does being serious. As does thinking in circles."

Lyse's shoulders slumped. "Gods, I'm not that bad…am I?"

Y'shtola settled the matter by serving her another slice.

"Should you doubt yourself, do not hesitate to lean on those around you. Upon us. You have more than the memories of your family to call upon, Lyse. Remember that."

Thus reminded, Lyse found her smile again.

While attending to the contents of her well-populated plate, Lyse reported on the recent happenings in her life.

"I've made a new friend," she began, through a mouthful of tart. "A boy about my age, who used to be in the Resistance. He...*mmm*...knows everything there is to know about Ala Mhigan politics and history—all the stuff I'm hopeless with, basically. It's...*mmm*...actually thanks to him that I had time to come here today. He helped me dig up some old records on a mine I'd been searching for." She paused mid-chew, eyebrows furrowed. "But he has this queer habit of looking straight past me. I thought he might have a lazy eye at first, but no—he just won't meet my gaze. I don't know what to make of it."

"I expect he's daunted," Alisaie posited. "And small wonder. You're a hero."

Y'shtola rolled her eyes. "Children, children...must I spell it out? The boy is smitten with you."

Lyse greeted this revelation with a shower of crumbs, and no small amount of coughing.

"You're joking!" she finally managed.

"Yes. I am famed for my sense of humor," Y'shtola agreed, her face stony. "But were that not the case, you might entertain the thought. Unless, of course, your heart is already spoken for? The handsome young lord of Doma was of a similar age, was he not?"

"What, H-Hien?! No! I don't— I mean, I admire him and all, but so do lots of people. And I might know someone who admires him especially."

Lyse's gaze floated off into the distance along with her thoughts. She said no more on the subject, and the others did not pry. As if to signal the end of her report, she gave her lemonade a hearty stir before narrowing her eyes at Y'shtola.

"What about you, Y'shtola? What do you think of, uh..." Lyse searched about for a suitable candidate, "Thancred, maybe? Or…one of the others?"

"I can honestly say that they have never crossed my mind. If you must know, however…"

At that moment, a memory came to her unbidden.

She was convalescing at the Rising Stones after her disastrous encounter with Zenos when her sister paid a visit. Though glad of her preservation, this latest brush with death had plainly come too soon after the Lifestream episode for Y'mhitra's liking, and she proceeded to rebuke her over the willful disregard she had shown for her own well-being. Her sister knew how dedicated she was to her chosen path, and would ordinarily have left it at a few stern words, but this time they burst forth as a torrent, knowing no cease until she sent Y'mhitra away, pleading fatigue. It was then that her sister had wearily spoken the words…

"Is it not past time you found someone? Strong you may be, but how much stronger might you prove with another at your side?"

The words resounded in Y'shtola's mind as she drained her tea. Beyond the cup, she spied the other two leaning forward in ill-concealed anticipation. She flashed them a curt smile.

"Nay. Mayhap it is better that I keep my own counsel."

Lyse and Alisaie fell back with a groan and set about grumbling. Ignoring them, Y'shtola reached for the teapot. Her hand stopped short as her ears discerned familiar footfalls.

"'Twould seem our gathering is finally complete."

In unison, the three Scions turned to look. And sure enough, it was him—the Warrior of Light.

"So, shall we order more of everything?"

The afternoon was yet young.

Tales from the Storm

The First Step

The mood in the Flames carriage was worthy of a wake. While pretending to gaze out at the parched landscape of southern Thanalan, the youth tried in vain to think of something to say. Across from him sat the grand company's recently formed summoner squad, the doughty souls charged with combatting primal threats—none of whom had said a word since their departure. Silently, he rehearsed an opening line. *So—you lot brave or stupid or both?*

Although he and his had been dispatched to render aid in this mission, they had yet to establish a rapport with the soldiers, and he was determined to break the ice.

"My name's Arenvald. Arenvald Lentinus," he eventually managed. And when no response was forthcoming, he added, "So—you lot…fight primals often?"

At this, the Lalafellin summoner sitting opposite shrugged wordlessly. *Why do I bother…* But then the woman next to him took pity and replied.

"As often as circumstances warrant, I suppose. Crispin and I have battled Ifrit four times now," she said, gesturing at the third summoner, who gamely accepted the conversational baton.

"Though our experience pales in comparison to the lieutenant's. Jajasamu is formerly of the Company of Heroes—he faced the Lord of Crags and lived."

Ah, so he's the dab hand. The lieutenant glanced at him briefly before looking away again, indifferent. *Probably wondering why you're riding with a pair of young nobodies.*

"Veterans, then? That's a relief. I'll try not to get underfoot."

As soon as the words had left his mouth, he regretted playing the part.

"Useless bloody whelps. If ye value yer life, ye'll do two things: watch and learn," Jajasamu snapped, before resuming his pre-battle ritual of ignoring one and all.

So that's the way it's going to be, eh? Arenvald stifled a sigh and forced a smile as he glanced sidelong at his fellow whelp, praying to the Twelve that she wouldn't make matters worse. But if the lieutenant's words had struck a nerve, she didn't show it. Her eyes were closed, her face devoid of all tension, the very picture of serenity. *The calm before the storm.*

Maybe the two of them have the right of it.

Accepting defeat, Arenvald abandoned his brilliant plan to befriend the squad before the battle, and instead cast his mind back to the circumstances that had led him to share a carriage with the summoners and Fordola Lupis.

Fate and the Scions had conspired to bring him back to Ala Mhigo, his homeland, and it was there that they had first met—as mortal enemies on the battlefield. The same age, the same birthplace, and yet somehow they had come to lead such different lives. He, the half-breed spawn of a Garlean soldier, cast out by his mother, had left Gyr Abania and become an adventurer, while she, a pureblood daughter of Ala Mhigo, had been gifted an imperial education and taken up arms against her own countrymen.

Yet for everything we strove to escape, to deny, our paths led us here.

As a Scion, he had earned the respect of the Resistance and the Ala Mhigan people, whereas she, as a traitor and a kinslayer, had earned their scorn. Only death would answer death, they believed—nor, perhaps, were they wrong.

And then came the day they stood on the same side of a battlefield.

Representatives had gathered from all across Gyr Abania to discuss the future of Ala Mhigo, only for proceedings to be plunged into chaos by Ananta treachery. Sri Lakshmi, summoned by the Qalyana, would have bound all present to her will, were it not for the intervention of the Warrior of Light, Arenvald…and Fordola.

"It's done. Take me back to my cell."

With those words, Fordola had thrown down the sword Lyse Hext put in her hands when the former Scion had challenged the hated Butcher to take her own life—as Zenos had—or use her newfound powers for a noble purpose. Arenvald watched them lead her away, watched as they once more debated the fate of his kinswoman and her fellow collaborators. In the end, it was Raubahn who had proffered the solution: conscription. A new unit in which some convicts might serve out their sentence instead of in a cell or at the end of a rope.

Though others were extended the offer, it was plain who they wanted most. Fordola had proven herself capable of withstanding primal influence. Her abilities as a Resonant, coupled with her combat expertise, made her an invaluable asset in the never-ending war against the primals.

A weapon.

She agreed.

"Out of the carriage! Let's go, let's go!"

The words of the Roegadyn captain riding with the coachman dragged Arenvald back to present. With practiced precision, the summoners grabbed their gear and disembarked, forming a line before their superior. Arenvald followed suit.

"As you know, yesterday, Master Coultenet of the Scions informed us of an aetheric disturbance in the vicinity of the Zanr'ak altar. Said disturbance can almost certainly be attributed to a primal summoning." The captain walked up and down the line, searching his soldiers' faces. "Luckily for us, we've got ourselves a couple of secret weapons."

Arenvald felt their eyes upon him and Fordola.

"Arenvald of the Scions, and Fordola of the Resistance. Echo-blessed, the both of them, so no need to worry about them getting tempered. That said, I'm obliged to divulge certain details regarding the latter..."

He saw their faces darken as they listened—their eyes narrow, their bodies tense. Fordola cocked her head and chuckled. "If I was going to stab you, it'd be from the front, not the back. But don't worry your little heads—my neck's still in the hangman's noose."

She tapped the gem-inlaid choker below her chin with two fingers. *You can trust in words or you can trust in magick.* If the Resistance thaumaturge tasked with keeping an eye on Fordola was so inclined, he could trigger the enchantment woven into the neckpiece, causing it to gradually grow warmer and tighter, slowly searing her skin as it choked the life from her. *Rather you than me. A proper hanging'd snap your neck, at least.*

The captain cleared his throat and continued. "Given their talents, we'll have them hold Ifrit at bay while the summoner squad engages at range with egi and magicks. You'll have healers as support, as well as the girl's minder. I'll be directing the diversionary maneuvers to the south. Any questions? Right, then."

They left the Forgotten Springs en masse and ventured a few malms east into the Sagolii, before Captain Wolf and his contingent peeled off to lay siege to a nearby Amalj'aa encampment, providing the summoner squad with the distraction they needed to head north towards the Zanr'ak altar undetected. Arenvald then led the way through a narrow canyon, clinging to the shadows some fifty yalms ahead of the party. Spying an oblivious sentry, he gestured for his comrades to stop, and slowly drew his dagger...

Wiping the blade clean, he looked back and signaled the others to join him. As one, they continued north towards the altar, where they found, as they had feared, a ring of flame, and the Lord of the Inferno waiting at its heart.

Even in the aftermath, he struggled to remember the fight.

The primal had been summoned with a token quantity of crystals, and Arenvald had not felt a fraction as hard-pressed as he had during the battle with Sri Lakshmi. The summoners and healers had all performed admirably. *A victory won on the training ground, not the battlefield.*

"We're finished here. All units, withdraw!" At Captain Wolf's command, they set out to return the way they had come.

"Advance no further!"

Arenvald was already diving the moment he heard the scream. Peering out from cover, he saw a figure in the dirt clutching an arrow in his gut, its black iron point protruding obscenely from his back. *Amalj'aa.*

"Stay put and stay quiet. Leave the fightin' to me and Aulie."

"Enemy archers, west ridge! Get behind those rocks!"

Arenvald closed his eyes, took a breath, and counted to four.

Shafts were raining down all around them now. Raising his shield, he broke and ran towards the summoners to help defend their retreat, and passed Fordola sprinting in the opposite direction, sword flashing as she danced through a hail of arrows.

"I knew it! I knew she'd run!" Jajasamu bellowed with a hint of triumph. Alarm bells ringing in his head, Arenvald looked back and saw she was headed for the wounded soldier—a Resistance man.

The thaumaturge.

But just as Arenvald felt his stomach drop into his boots and the grip of his sword dig deep into his palm, he saw Fordola pull the mage to his feet and offer him her shoulder. And then Arenvald was running again, this time into the open, his silver armor flashing in the sunlight as he shouted curses and threw stones at the archers on the ridge, daring them to face him.

After a time, the arrows subsided, and the archers vanished from sight. *Better to leave the madman be, eh?* For a moment, he let himself relax.

"Keep your guard up, boy!"

Arenvald caught the first arrow on his shield and drew his sword in time to cut down the second and third. "Sorry, A'aba," he whispered. The archer, a hulking brute of an Amalj'aa wearing a mask, took careful aim. *Bugger it.*

With a cry he raised his shield and charged, closing the gap and driving his full weight into his ill-prepared foe. As the archer staggered backward, Arenvald raised his sword and brought it down, cleaving his enemy's bow in two as he raised it in a vain attempt to ward off the blow. The Amalj'aa crumpled to the earth, and the surrounding sand grew dark and wet. The silence was deafening, and Arenvald knew the champion's comrades had been watching.

"Bloody hells, that was the stupidest display of 'heroism' I've seen in years. And they wonder why I hate the young ones…"

Muttering under his breath, the summoner bade his familiar return to him. As the floating mass of rock passed Arenvald, he saw the masked Amalj'aa's final arrow was lodged squarely in its breast.

The mood in the Flames carriage was worthy of a nameday feast, the summoners all smiles as they chatted amongst themselves and even laughed at some of Arenvald's jokes. Fordola sat apart from it all, elbows on knees, head bowed, though the Scion thought he spied Jajasamu giving her an appraising look.

Before they had set out, Arenvald had been with her when the thaumaturge wandered over. She had been kneeling in the sand, packing up her gear when he asked why she had risked her life to save his. "Little girls need their fathers," was all she said, before tightening a final strap and boarding the carriage.

The man had turned to him then, his face a picture of perplexity. "I never said anything about having a daughter."

To which Arenvald could only shrug and smile. "Lucky guess."

It all begins with the first step.

Tales from the Storm

Ever After

Beneath a blue sky unmarred by even a single errant cloud, the people of the enclave went about their business with the faintest hint more energy than usual. Perhaps they took strength from the undeniable progress they had made in rebuilding their broken home, brick by brick, stone by stone. Perhaps it was the presence of the imperial conscripts recently returned to Doma, and their tearful loved ones. Or perhaps it was simply the gentle sunlight that warmed body and soul alike. *Wherever you are, Gosetsu, I pray your burdens are lighter this day.*

Yugiri was bound for the Ten Thousand Stalls to collect a ledger of sales and imports on behalf of Lord Hien. As was all too often the case, Doma's young lord had naively believed that he would be capable of doing so himself, only to be waylaid by retainers and petitioners the moment he set foot outside his door. Though a part of her balked at the idea of leaving him to the mercy of the mob, she knew that no harm would come to her master so long as Hakuro remained at his side. Still, she could not help but worry, for Lord Hien's insistence on speaking directly with his people, while admirable, took up far too much of his time, and it was only through weeks of dogged persistence that she and the others had finally convinced him to delegate some few of his routine responsibilities.

As she drew closer to the stalls, however, she realized that today would be anything but routine, for a massive winged beast the color of the dusk sat patiently in the nearby square. Though the townsfolk seemed distinctly uncertain, she knew it for what it was: a tamed yol of the Steppe. *But not Hien's... A visitor's, then?*

I swear, if the Buduga have come looking for their man again...

But the tension coiled within her began to subside the moment she saw the young woman bartering with a nearby greengrocer. The young woman to whom she owed an unrepayable debt for saving her liege lord's life.

"Cirina? What brings you to the enclave this day?"

"Yugiri! Pray forgive me my unannounced visit..."

At the behest of Temulun Khatun, the young udgan explained, she had ventured forth from Mol Iloh in search of rare herbs for a feast. The old gods were fond of such commandments, it would seem, but on this occasion she had been unable to procure the necessary ingredients from any of the merchants in Reunion. After making further inquiries, Cirina had learned that the herbs she sought were native to Yanxia, and where else would one find myriad foodstuffs but the Ten Thousand Stalls of the Doman Enclave?

"Heavy rains delayed the latest shipment, but the trader expects it to arrive today. She left but a moment ago for the docks…"

"I see. Full glad am I to hear your troubles will soon be over."

"Oh, it really hasn't been so difficult…"

As Cirina trailed off, the pair found themselves in the midst of an inevitable silence. *Say something.* Yugiri saw her own discomfort mirrored by the young udgan, who gripped one arm above the elbow and struggled to meet her gaze. She considered taking her leave—she had official duties to attend to, after all—but decided against it. Cirina was a stranger to this place, and the least she could do was keep the poor girl company until her business was concluded.

"I…I have been meaning to ask. About Lord Hien—" She paused involuntarily, noticing Cirina's frozen expression. *Say something else.* "About how the two of you first met, and how your people nursed him back to health. Mayhap you could share the tale with me while you wait?"

At this, Cirina visibly relaxed, an eager smile spreading across her face. "Yes, yes of course!" she exclaimed, nodding for good measure.

And so the pair retired to a nearby table where Cirina set about recounting how the fates of the peoples of Yanxia and the Steppe had been intertwined and forever changed.

"It can be difficult at times to discern the meaning of the old gods' whispers, but when they spoke to Grandmother that day, their intent was clear. ''Twixt Steppe and wood, where land meets sky, a kingdom's fate hangs by a thread.' I led a group of Mol past Reunion and into the mountains between our lands and yours. We knew not for what we searched, nor where we should look, but in the end we were guided to a small clearing in the wood, where we found a Doman dressed in tatters, caked with mud and dried blood. He was surely dead, I thought, and in that moment I feared I had failed…until I saw his fingers twitch.

"I rushed to his side and began tending to his hurts while calling out to the others—quietly, for I suspected he had been cut down in his flight from the ironmen, and we were ill-prepared to fight. When we felt it was safe to move him, we bore him to our horses and rode straight for Mol Iloh.

"He lay unconscious for days, in the grip of a terrible fever. So grievous were his wounds that we feared he would never recover. Some questioned the wisdom of us sheltering this stranger from the war-torn south, this Doman whom they suspected was a leader of men. But Grandmother would not suffer any talk of casting him out. He would be nursed back to health, and in time all our questions would be answered. None would gainsay her wisdom in this, of course, though some yet harbored doubts.

"All the while, he lay thrashing about in his sleep, crying out for his father again and again. Wailing… He had watched him die, I knew— knew it in my heart. His grief was primal, all-consuming, and I could not bear to listen…but nor could I bear to leave him alone. Never before had I heard a man make such sounds. Never again do I wish to."

Cirina paused, her eyes taking in a moment long since passed. *I may envy you some things, but I do not envy you this.*

"Some days were better than others. He languished there, drifting in and out of consciousness, for more than a month, until one day, quite without warning, he stumbled from his room and fell to his knees before Grandmother and me, muttering something. At first, I thought his strength spent, but then I saw how he pressed his forehead to the earth and heard him thank us for granting him succor. I begged him to rise, said there was no need for such formality, but he remained as he was and continued.

"It was then that he told us he was Hien, son of Kaien. Lord of Doma.

"He feared that imposing upon us further might invite imperial reprisals, but Grandmother refused to listen. He was Mol now—family—and one does not simply abandon family. She implored him to rest and regain his strength, for he would need all that and more for the trials ahead. As for his secrets, they were ours now. None would betray his trust.

"Not that he had any cause to fear betrayal or discovery. The ironmen had never taken an interest in the Steppe. So Hien was free to come and go as he pleased—to retrain his body through the many tasks he insisted we leave to him. Simple chores, for the most part, though he struggled much with them in the beginning, as his hands and feet betrayed him in unexpected ways. Yet we never saw him succumb to frustration. Instead, he would chuckle at his own clumsiness, and promise to do better. At least, this was the face he presented to us when he knew we were near. When he did not..."

Again Cirina paused, her breath held in her throat, as if she were suddenly uncertain.

"I spied upon him once as he practiced with his sword away from the camp. When it slipped from his fingers, he froze, arms still held out before him. I could see him panting with the effort, make out the sweat running down his neck... Slowly he looked to his hands, and as he stood there closing them into fists and opening them again, he looked almost...lost."

Aren't we all.

"Yet he recovered. Grew faster and stronger with each passing day, until he was more than a match for any Mol. He earned his keep and the trust of all, and those difficult times were soon forgotten. It was tempting to pretend he had always been with us, and always would be, but...

"One evening I went in search of him, to call him home to eat. I found him, as I knew I would, at his usual spot atop a small rise, looking out over the Steppe. He would often sit there in silence, and until that day I had never thought to wonder why. But there in the fading light, I finally understood. He looked not on the Steppe, but to the distant lands beyond it. To the south.

"I was always reluctant to intrude upon these moments. Doubly so then. But having glimpsed the future in the bloodred sunset, I knew I must. And so I edged closer and called out, 'When you return to them, what will you do?'

"With eyes still fixed on the southern horizon, and not the slightest hint of surprise, he replied, 'Should they yet thirst for freedom—should they yet yearn to stand and fight, then I shall be their sword and lead them in my father's stead. But should their thirst be quenched by the bitter draught of defeat—should they have had their fill of blood and ash, then I shall be their reprieve.'

"I was tempted in that moment. 'Stay, then—leave them to their peace, and you to yours here.' Selfish and impossible and sure to be refused, but the words were on my lips…and in my heart."

Saying this, Cirina looked Yugiri in the eye, daring her to speak. But she said nothing; only inclined her head a fraction. *Go on…*

"The Mol are few in number. We know every face, every name—we know what it means to fight for one another. But nations and kingdoms such as yours are different. These identities and ideals to which you swear allegiance, for which you fight and die are foreign to us. But I think perhaps it is the same for Mol and the old gods. There are things we cannot see nor touch that nevertheless have value. Things in which we place our faith, and from which we derive strength, and without which we are…incomplete.

"After explaining his intent, Hien rose and came to me, apologizing for keeping me from my dinner. We walked together in silence for a time, until I took his hand in mine—"

Cirina swallowed her words and looked away, prompting Yugiri to realize she had been staring intently at the young woman. She blinked and affected an air of calm composure before motioning for Cirina to continue.

"I couldn't tell you why, really. I was just as surprised as he was. But I think…I think I wanted him to know how I felt. So I told him—"

What's done is done.

"Told him that we should go hunting the next day. And the day after that. That he might grow stronger than he was—so that when the war was rejoined, he could lead his people to victory."

Oh.

"Some men are not destined for quiet lives. Hien would fight for his homeland till his dying breath—like his father before him. And so, his path being set, all I could hope to do was help him walk it to its end.

"Having said my piece, I let go. Our hands drifted apart…though for the briefest of moments, our fingertips held firm—"

Oh?

"But in the end, I let him go.

"With a bold, beautiful smile, he said it was a wonderful idea, and looked forward to following my lead. And then we went home and ate with the others."

Her tale concluded, Cirina placed her hands in her lap and took a breath. "So you see, when you finally came for him, I could not have been happier. For his people still yearned to fight. His gods had not finished with him yet."

Yugiri simply nodded in reply. *An admirable effort, that smile. And the rest.* The young woman had taken Lord Hien's measure, and rightly judged that his true love would always be Doma. *Yet the mind and the heart are not always in accord. Some feelings may never be reconciled, and on warm days and cold nights, our thoughts may wander to what could have been…*

The trader chose then to make his return. The coveted herbs had indeed arrived, and Cirina was presented with a basketful for her needs. After exchanging words and payment, the udgan turned back to Yugiri.

"Well! I should be on my way. Thank you for keeping me company."

"The pleasure was mine, but…are you sure you do not wish to stay awhile longer? To speak with Lord Hien, perhaps? I am certain he would be glad to see you."

"No, no. I expect he is very busy attending to his people's needs, and since I have nothing important to discuss… In fact, you needn't tell him I was here at all."

Again, Cirina flashed a smile. *Really…* Yugiri scowled inwardly. *We shall see about that.*

"Ah, forgive me. I recall now that there was an urgent matter to which I had to attend—"

It was true, to be fair, but when she broke into a run, her official duties were the furthest thing from her mind. Darting through the streets of the enclave, she whipped her head back and forth, looking down every side street. Running, searching, running, searching. *Right or wrong, selfish or impossible…*

There he was, surrounded by the usual entourage. Yugiri pushed through the crowd with ungentle force. "Lord Hien! *Lord Hien!*"

"Yugiri? Whatever's gotten into you?"

"Ci…Cirina is here, in the enclave. She came to purchase some herbs, but if you hurry—"

Her words were drowned out by the piercing cry of a yol soaring overhead. All eyes were drawn to the silhouette crossing the sun, before bird and rider veered northward and began to fade into the blue. *Damn it.*

"…She is well?"

Lord Hien's eyes were still fixed on the cloudless sky. Lingering on the limitless possibilities. *But duty comes before all.*

"Quite well, my lord. Which is why she did not wish to trouble you."

For an instant, something flashed across his face. *A son, broken and mended, flexing weakened fingers. He looked almost…lost.*

"Would that she had and granted me some much-needed respite! But then I would be that much more delayed, so perhaps it is for the best." With a wry smile, he whirled round to face the waiting crowd. "Right, then! All your petitions will be heard, so please wait patiently for your turn."

And just like that, he was the Lord of Doma again.

The Samurai Who Couldn't Die

"By your leave!"

Gosetsu lowered himself down somewhat gingerly next to a weathered skull, crossing his aching legs as he glanced about the surrounding field. Since shaving his head and setting off on a pilgrimage to honor the fallen, the former samurai's winding road had led him to the border of Ilsabard. It was here, some two decades past, that a battle had raged between the forces of the Empire and the peoples of a subjugated province. The remains of the vanquished still lay unburied, discolored bones protruding from the undulating sea of wildgrass.

"I know not who you were, friend, nor yet for whom you fought, but I do know you were a warrior."

The Roegadyn paused politely, as if affording the skull time to respond.

When it did not, he continued, "Here you lie, moldering away with none to mourn your passing, while this old man clings shamelessly to life. And yet, in my defense, none could say that I have not afforded the kami *ample* opportunity to claim this tired soul…"

It had been twenty-five years since his first appointment with death…

Gosetsu had fought like a demon against the invading Empire, but even a man of his indomitable will could not prevail against the might of Garlemald. Defeated, both he and his lord Kaien were taken prisoner, their beloved Doma falling at last to imperial rule.

Disgraced and dishonored by his capture, the breaking of his spirit was completed by the news of his family's fate: his wife and daughter had perished during the imperial bombardment of Monzen. In dedicating every waking moment to his liege, Gosetsu had all but left his spouse to run their household alone. And on no few occasions had he come home to find his five-year-old asleep in the doorway, where she had waited to welcome her father's return. He had often considered begging leave from his duties that he might spend time with his loved ones, but now even that humble wish would never be granted.

Robbed of his will to live, Gosetsu thought only of being reunited in death. His life, however, was not his own to take—unable to beg Kaien's consent, the samurai was forced to endure the agony of his imprisonment. Six moons waxed and waned before one day, without warning, the guards strode into his cell and dragged him from his meager bedding.

Wordlessly, they led him to a nearby chamber, wherein waited Doma's former ruler. It seemed their captors had at last permitted Kaien a visitor; but rather than ask for his beloved wife, he had requested to speak with his most loyal retainer. Even as the door closed behind him, Gosetsu fell to his knees and begged for the right to commit *seppuku*. But Kaien simply closed his eyes, and shook his head.

"Why?!" Gosetsu rasped, his voice hoarse from disuse. "Why do you deny me this small mercy?!"

Kaien was not only his master, but his oldest and dearest friend. Rarely did the samurai question his lord's decisions, but in the face of this unfeeling refusal, he could not conceal his dismay.

"Our nation has fallen. My family is dead. I failed to protect all that is dear to me! Honor demands that I turn my blade—"

"I need you alive," came the reply, silencing Gosetsu at a stroke. "I trust no other to watch over my son. None."

This was the first Gosetsu had heard of an heir. In the pandemonium that followed the Empire's invasion, Kaien explained, he had told no one that his wife, Mina, was with child—a boy, if the predictions of the onmyoji were to be believed. The revelation left Gosetsu agog. *He will come into a world of strife and subjugation. If I do not stand at his side, then who will?*

Tears welling in his eyes, the samurai withdrew his earlier request, and swore to his liege a new oath. He would not fail this time.

"So it was that my first death was denied," Gosetsu explained to his mute audience. "His son, Shun, was born soon after, and I was conscripted to fight the Empire's battles for them. To draw a blade in service of another—of our hated enemy, no less—was a humiliation worse than dying, but such was the price of remaining true to my oath. I turned my heart to stone, and carved a bloody trail with my steel. Full many fell before me...some on this very battlefield." Gosetsu regarded the skull sympathetically. "Were you one of them, I understand if your spirit chose to haunt me. Such terrible deeds I performed in the name of honor..."

Hollow eye sockets stared back at him, but no vengeful specter stirred within their depths. The old Roegadyn plunged onwards with his recollections.

"Which brings me to the recent uprising, and what should have been my second death…"

It was the twenty-fourth winter of the imperial occupation. Lord Kaien had been permitted to retake his place as Doma's leader—a puppet made to dance to Garlemald's tune. His wife Mina, meanwhile, had passed away, the long years of anguish taking their toll. As for the young Shun, he had grown into an exceptional warrior, taking the name "Hien" following his coming-of-age ceremony. And Gosetsu himself had returned to serve House Rijin, playing up old wounds as a means to escape further service on the front lines.

Though each gave the impression of a man resigned to his fate, the truth could not have been more different. In secret, the trio had spent countless nights plotting Doma's liberation, going so far as to establish a base of resistance in the House of the Fierce. And yet, after almost a quarter of a century of imperial rule, the time to rise up seemed no closer.

But then word arrived that the Emperor had succumbed to old age, and that a war of succession was brewing in Garlemald. The kami themselves could not have presented a better opportunity. Waiting patiently until the local garrison had been dispatched to join the conflict back in the motherland, Gosetsu led a rebel force to lay siege to Doma Castle, and after a brief battle, both it and the viceroy lay in Doman hands.

Yet as swiftly as their victory had come, still more swiftly came the Empire's retribution. The internecine struggle within the capital was resolved sooner than any had thought possible, and reinforcements dispatched to Doma forthwith. Arriving at the head of the XIIth Legion, the newly anointed Emperor's own son—the crown prince Zenos—fell upon the rebels like a tidal wave. Overwhelmed, Gosetsu abandoned the castle to the flood of imperial troops, seeking at least to uphold his word by ensuring Hien's survival. They had scarcely reached safety when they learned of Lord Kaien's fate: while attempting to coordinate the evacuation of his people, Doma's ruler was confronted by Zenos and slain in single combat.

"I will avenge him!" Gosetsu vowed then. "Even should mine own life be the price of vengeance!" Gripping the hilt of his katana, the grief-maddened samurai prepared to charge into the enclave where the XIIth had set up camp, only for Hien to bar his path.

"I share your grief at Father's passing," the young man said, his expression stern. "But we must pull back and await our next chance at freedom. I am your lord now," he continued, not unkindly, "and I order you to withdraw."

For a moment, Gosetsu's body went rigid, but then he allowed his hand to fall away from his weapon. His liege and closest friend was dead. Caring not who might be watching, he fell to his knees and wept.

"And thus was the underworld denied my eternal soul once more. I ask you—what manner of samurai lives to tell the tale of his lord's demise?" A rueful grin spread across Gosetsu's broad features. "One would be forgiven for questioning my loyalties…"

Shaking his head, he let out a deep sigh.

"Where was I? Ah, yes—following our defeat, we were compelled to remain ever on the move, striking at our enemy whenever the opportunity arose. But while evading some particularly persistent pursuers, we became separated. I searched, of course. Oh, how I searched. But my liege was nowhere to be found. And so I left for Eorzea to enlist the aid of Yugiri Mistwalker.

"To cut a long story short," Gosetsu went on, cheerfully, "we were eventually reunited with our young lord, at whose side we marched upon Doma Castle once more. And 'twas there that I came to stare into the eyes of death for the third time.

"Our foe, you see, foreseeing our victory, had made arrangements to bring the keep down on our heads. Yet even as the masonry crumbled around me, I was content to perish in the knowledge that Lord Hien was safe and Doma free. 'Twould have been a good end. Mayhap the best. But once again, the kami proved reluctant to grant me my final rest…"

Gosetsu had awoken to find himself drifting down the One River atop a stout wooden door whose twisted hinges had chanced to snag upon his sleeve—nor was he alone. By some miracle, Yotsuyu too had been spared. Yet despite his hatred for the viceroy, he could not strike at her as she lay there senseless. Instead, he spent his strength on keeping their precarious raft from tipping as the current carried them out into the open sea.

They washed up on the beach of a small island, where Yotsuyu at last regained consciousness. She seemed confused by the situation—unable even to recall her own name. Gosetsu naturally suspected trickery, but when he advanced upon her, blade drawn, she dissolved into fits of frightened weeping. In that moment, he saw not the viceroy, but the face of his lost little girl, cheeks streaked with tears after a scolding. The point of his katana dropped into the sand. He could no more cut her down than he could his own daughter.

So began their time as castaways. What would have been torture for some—surviving on rainwater and the few fish that could be caught—seemed to Gosetsu a tranquil dream after a lifetime of conflict. Yotsuyu spoke to him as an honored grandfather, seeking his approval with an innocence that touched his heart. And as affection blossomed unbidden, he in turn began thinking of her as a grandchild. The spiteful woman he had once cursed as his foe gradually ceased to be.

"Ayame…? Is that who I am?"

One morning, still drowsy from sleep, Gosetsu had mistaken the wide-eyed Yotsuyu for his long-dead daughter. Stricken with guilt, he had then resolved to make a conscious effort to call her "Tsuyu." Yet the similarity could not be denied… *Had Ayame lived, she would have been of a similar age…* And just like that, Gosetsu caught himself contemplating a life on the little island, and simply forgetting all that had gone before.

But he was beholden to his duty: his lord must know that he and Yotsuyu had survived. And so, as soon as his wounds permitted, Gosetsu chopped down their sanctuary's solitary tree, fashioned a crude raft, and began paddling towards the nearest shore…

"My reunion with Lord Hien was joyous enough, but I must confess my heart was filled with trepidation," the old Roegadyn said softly. "I feared what judgment he would pronounce on Tsuyu. But my liege is a merciful man, and he granted her leave to live among us as a Doman citizen until such time as her memories returned.

"In my elation, I convinced myself that everything that had come to pass—our miraculous survival; my inability to wield a blade—was a sign from the kami that I was destined to spend the rest of my days at Tsuyu's side. Fond fool... That I of all men should presume to understand the will of the divine."

Gosetsu stared into the distance, eyes clouded with anguish.

"Sure enough, Yotsuyu's true self returned, her crimes inviting an inevitable death. Tsuyu was gone, and I was left to mourn once more."

His story told, he bowed his head and lapsed into silence. The skull, however, seemed unmoved. Marking its impassive expression, Gosetsu laughed quietly.

"Mine apologies. I did not come here to bore you with an old man's tales. I came to see that you and your comrades are given the proper rites."

So saying, he heaved himself to his feet, and began the laborious process of burying each and every bone that littered the field. That task complete, he constructed a simple cairn of stones, and read aloud a passage of prayer in reverent tones. And then he collapsed.

Gosetsu awoke to find himself sitting at the prow of a small ferry, enveloped in a nimbus of warm light. The craft bobbed in the waters of a broad river, and upon the far bank he could make out a small gathering of people, beckoning him to cross. Squinting at their faces, he made out his wife and daughter, and his dear friend Kaien. Even Tsuyu was there, smiling again. Gosetsu smiled back. *At long last, death has come to embrace me.*

"I shall be with you soon!" he called out, snatching up the oar lying across the vessel's bench, and starting to paddle in earnest. Yet however furiously he churned the water, the ferry would not move forward. He looked up to see the distant bank drawing ever farther away. Desperate now, Gosetsu flung aside the oar, and dove into the river...

The next thing he knew, he felt solid ground beneath his back. A peddler, judging by his attire, was leaning over him, peering worriedly into his eyes.

"Had yourself a bit of a turn, did you?" the man asked kindly, enunciating each syllable for ease of comprehension. "I have some spare food and water, if you think you can stomach it?"

"A turn…?" Gosetsu replied groggily. "Where is Ayame…? Tsuyu…?" His thoughts swirled in confusion, until a rumbling growl from his belly reminded him where he was and what he had been doing.

For three days and three nights he had toiled in the field, without so much as a sip of water or a grain of rice passing his lips. Unsure whether to feel embarrassed or saddened by his predicament, Gosetsu resolved instead to see the mirth in it.

"I thought for certain my time had come, but 'twould seem the kami are not done with me yet," he chuckled. "So be it! If I am to remain in this world, then I shall greet every precious moment as a dear friend. What more can a man do but smile?"

With a customarily earsplitting laugh, Gosetsu took the proffered bread from the startled merchant's hands, and wolfed it down in three hurried bites. He would need his strength if he was to continue his pilgrimage.

There is a power in these stories, I believe, for they are more than the creations of a creative mind—they are truth, personal and real. The struggles, the triumphs, and the failures of these people resonate with me deeply, and with many of you, I suspect.

But perhaps the most riveting, most moving tales of our hero and his comrades come after. The tales of that tumultuous chapter that would follow, when Light's champion would fall to—nay, embrace abyssal Dark. As all know well.

Alas, no matter how much I wish it were not so, the wondrous and strange adventures upon which our hero ⦵⦵⦵⦵⦵⦵⦵⦵⦵⦵⦵⦵⦵⦵⦵⦵

May it never end
The struggle and the story

A Note on the Contents

With the exception of the four written for this compilation, these stories were first published on the official FINAL FANTASY XIV website, the Lodestone. They have been further edited and reformatted for print.

FINAL FANTASY XIV
Chronicles of Light

Planning & Production
Square Enix Co., Ltd.
Editor-in-Chief: Kazuhiro Oya
Editors: Tomoko Hatakeyama, Takuji Tada
Production: Toru Karasawa, Toshihiro Ohoka, Tsutomu Sakai

Writers
Banri Oda, Natsuko Ishikawa, Daichi Hiroi, Yuki Kimura, John Crow, Naoki Yoshida

Cover & Interior Illustrations
Toshiyuki Itahana

English Translation
John Crow, Phil Bright, Kenneth Pinyopusarerk, John Townsend, Agness Kaku

English Editor
Morgan Morris Rushton

Special Thanks
Michael-Christopher Koji Fox, Nao Matsuda, Asami Matsumoto
FINAL FANTASY XIV Development Team

Book Design & DTP
QBIST Inc. (QBIST)
Yukiko Yamada, Moe Muraki

Supervision
FINAL FANTASY XIV Producer & Director Naoki Yoshida

First published in Japan in 2019 by SQUARE ENIX CO., LTD.
English translation © 2019 SQUARE ENIX CO., LTD.
All Rights Reserved. Published in the United States by Square Enix Books, an imprint of the Book Publishing Division of SQUARE ENIX, INC.

ISBN: 978-1-64609-185-0

Library of Congress Cataloging-in-Publication data is on file with the publisher.

Printed in the U.S.A.
First printing, October 2022
10 9 8 7 6 5 4 3 2 1

SQUARE ENIX
BOOKS

www.square-enix-books.com

[North America]
Square Enix, Inc.
999 N Sepulveda Blvd., 3rd Floor
El Segundo, CA 90245, USA